STRANGER TO HER HEART

"It's a simple life here," Wynne pointed out.

Scott smiled. "I've noticed. I like your island, Wynne. I like it very much."

They walked back to the hotel. Under a palm tree near the front entrance, Scott paused. He reached out and took her by the shoulders. He seemed very tall, very attentive, very attractive in the half-light.

"Good-night, Wynne."

He kissed her. She was startled and yet did nothing to stop him. His lips were warm and hungry. It was pleasant. But no more. He sensed this.

"Someday, Wynne Russell, you're going to kiss me the way I want you to kiss me!"

PROMISE OF TOMORROW
An Arlene Hale Romance

Promise of Tomorrow
Arlene Hale

BANTAM BOOKS · TORONTO · NEW YORK · LONDON

FOR DALE, THE FLORIDIAN

The characters in this story are fictitious. Any resemblance to persons living or dead is purely coincidental.

This low-priced Bantam Book
has been completely reset in a type face
designed for easy reading, and was printed
from new plates. It contains the complete
text of the original hard-cover edition.
NOT ONE WORD HAS BEEN OMITTED.

PROMISE OF TOMORROW
*A Bantam Book / published by arrangement with
Little, Brown and Company*

PRINTING HISTORY
*Little, Brown edition published February 1973
2nd printing.....April 1973
Bantam edition / January 1975*

Bantam Books are published by Bantam Books, Inc. Its trademark, consisting of the words "Bantam Books" and the portrayal of a bantam, is registered in the United States Patent Office and in other countries. Marca Registrada. Bantam Books, Inc., 666 Fifth Avenue, New York, New York 10019.

PRINTED IN THE UNITED STATES OF AMERICA

I

IT WAS A BRIGHT, warm, June day. Tallahassee simmered under the sun, and Wynne Russell felt caged in her office. Beyond the window, she stared at the city below, and part of her longed to be free, barefoot, running across the white sand of Feather Island. She wanted to cross the lobby of the old South Wind Hotel and drop into her father's office for a chat with him. Later, join Lorrie for a long session of girl talk.

"Am I homesick?" she asked herself incredulously.

Perhaps. For the many good things she'd left on the island. But there was always the other side of the coin. Eric Channon still lived there in his beach house on Dolphin Bay. Eric with the sea green eyes and the black, thick hair and the smile that touched off rockets inside her.

Wynne made herself stop thinking about him. It was over. Done. For more than two years now. It was why she had left her work in Miami and come here. To be farther away. She no longer visited Feather Island for any length of time, and Tallahassee made spending weekends there impractical. Miami had been too close. She had wanted and needed distance between Eric and herself. But it was on days such as this that she felt a vague restlessness, an uneasiness, and found herself watching the clock, anxious to leave her office and the building, eager to be unleashed, uncaged.

The phone rang on her desk, and she snatched it up.

"Miss Wynne Russell?"

"Yes."

"This is Western Union. I have a telegram for you."

She gripped the telephone tightly and felt a wave of panic. Didn't telegrams usually mean trouble?

1

"It is from Priscilla Russell," said the voice on the other end of the wire.

Grandmother! She was truly alarmed now. Dad? Had something happened to Dad?

"The message reads, COME HOME AT ONCE."

"Is that all?" Wynne asked anxiously.

"Yes."

"I see. Thank you."

She hung up. Surely no one was ill. No one had died. If that had been the case, the wire would have been more explicit. This was exactly the way Grandmother did things! She was a hard taskmaster. The captain of her own ship. She had operated the South Wind Hotel with a firm hand for twenty-five years and had then turned it over to Dad a few years ago. Grandmother never leaned on anyone. But now, suddenly, she wanted Wynne to come home.

For a moment, rebellion welled up in Wynne's throat. Grandmother snapped her fingers and everyone jumped. What did the old woman have that compelled Wynne to go running at the drop of a hat? Then, with a resigned sigh, Wynne reached for the phone and called the airport. She made a reservation and then called her boss, Jack Brown, in his office down the hall. She explained what had happened.

"I hope it's nothing serious," Jack said.

"With my grandmother, everything is serious," Wynne said.

"How long will you be gone?" Jack asked.

"I don't know. I'll be in touch."

"All right, Wynne. Hurry back."

"Thanks, Jack. You're sweet."

"Ah, at last, a word of encouragement," Jack laughed.

She hung up. Jack Brown was nice. He headed the Brown Development Company and was responsible for one of the larger new housing developments in Tallahassee. Working with Jack was fun. Demanding. A challenge. He wanted bright, young people around him. He demanded the best they could give him. Wynne's job was to look at the whole picture as a woman would see it. One of the most popular houses in the last development had several touches for which she was responsible.

2

Jack had asked her out several times. She had gone occasionally, but sensing that he wanted to be serious, she had tried to discourage him. What did she have to offer anyone right now?

There was no time to linger. She took a cab home to her small apartment, packed a few things while the driver waited, and then went directly to the airport. She had twenty minutes to catch her plane for Fort Myers. From there, she would take a small plane to Charlton.

For a moment, a mental picture of the South Wind Hotel flashed across her eyes. The hotel had always been a part of her life in one way or another. She could see the bright green shutters, the glint of the sea just beyond, the wind-twisted palms, and hear the cry of the gulls, the swish of water rushing over the white sand.

It must be the hotel! Grandmother loved that old place. It had been her life for so long. But Dad was there at the helm. Efficient, well liked, well organized. What on earth—?

It was pointless to try and puzzle it out now. She would have to wait until she reached the island. Perhaps, with luck, she could return to Tallahassee tomorrow. The quicker the better. She didn't want to see anyone but family while she was there, except Lorrie. She always wanted to see Lorrie, her best friend. And Captain Sam, of course. She loved Sam with a kind of childish ardor. No one else. Please, no one else!

The flight to Fort Myers was a smooth one, and the short hop to Charlton was running late, but she made it to the ferry landing a few minutes before five. Captain Sam Engle's ferry, which he fondly called *The Lady*, was tied up there, but Captain Sam was nowhere about.

Wynne went aboard to wait. From here, she could see Feather Island, so called because its shape was somewhat like that of a long, curved, slender feather. Mangrove Sound separated it from the mainland, and on the far side, the Gulf waters swept over the sand and brought them, for the most part, ideal weather. And always a breeze.

A small truck lumbered up to the landing and came to a halt. She knew the old vehicle. There was a standing bet around the island as to when it would fall completely apart.

3

The man got out and paused to look around him, obviously impatient.

"Hello, Will!" Wynne called with a wave.

Will Dykes wore faded work clothes, an oil-stained cap and looked no younger or older than he ever had.

"That you, Wynne?"

"In the flesh," she answered. "Where's Sam?"

"Lallygagging around, I suppose. Always late with the five o'clock run. You'd think he'd run his business better than that, wouldn't you now?"

Wynne hid a frown. Will Dykes was not the most ambitious man in the world. He owned and operated the only garage on the island. Perhaps that gave him a certain superiority. He could make people wait while he took his own sweet time because there was no where else they could go. By comparison, Captain Sam was by far the better businessman. Sam kept a few rental boats, operated a ferry on a twice-a-day basis, along with special runs when needed, and saw to it that the mail was carried to and from the island. In his tiny little office building, he also ran a sub-post office.

"How's Lorrie?" Wynne asked. "I missed seeing her my last visit home."

Will made a face and scratched at his two-day-old beard and scowled. "That girl's going to be the death of me. Always got some crazy notion in her head. Always wantin' to run off to the mainland. Now what more could a girl want than what she's already got? A roof over her head, three squares a day, and the way I got things going for her up on the hill—she's sittin' pretty."

Wynne didn't know what Will was referring to. She only knew that Lorrie was an unhappy girl. Will wanted her on the island under his thumb. To keep the house and cook his meals and see to his needs. Not to mention the responsibility of raising young Johnny. But Lorrie was a free spirit, a gull on the wing, and Wynne knew how keenly she wanted to get off the island for good.

"Young people don't appreciate nothin' you do for them these days," Will grumbled. "And that's a fact!"

Wynne caught sight of a small, short figure, walking with a kind of rolling gait that partially disguised his limp. His skin was sun-weathered, and his eyes were always

4

the clearest of blue. They missed little. He wore faded clothes, a seaman's cap, and canvas shoes. Around any kind of boat he was as agile as a ten-year-old child, even with his lame leg.

"Here comes Sam," Wynne said with a smile.

Captain Sam Engle had a canvas mail sack slung over his shoulder. He nodded to Will Dykes, unfastened a chain, and motioned Will to drive his truck aboard.

"Hi, Sam," Wynne called.

Sam broke into a pleased grin. "Why, I never! Wynne. It's you!"

He grasped her hands in his for a moment and beamed at her from under the brim of his cap. She found herself caught up in his merry blue gaze. His pleasure at seeing her was genuine.

"How are you, Sam?"

"I'm like always. Home for a visit?"

"Something like that."

"By golly, I'm glad to see you. The island's just not the same without you!"

She gave him a hug. "That's for being such a sweet liar."

"Who's lying? Who's lying!" he fussed at her indignantly.

"For cryin' out loud, we goin' or not?" Will Dykes yelled at him.

Sam muttered something under his breath and prepared to get under way. Sam had taught Wynne a great deal. How to handle a small craft on stormy waters, how to look for rare shells, how to know when the fish were running, and all manner of things about the island. He'd given her a personal history course in World War II. He'd been in the thick of it. His lame leg was living proof of it.

"You got all day?" Will was shouting impatiently.

Sam, aggravated by now, tilted his cap back so that some of his white hair showed, and shouted back. "Matter of fact, I have!"

Wynne heard the car coming, fast, the horn sounding. Someone was running late and trying to catch the ferry before it left.

With a sinking sensation, Wynne knew who it was.

How could this have happened? She contemplated leaving the ferry to avoid him. But this was the last regular ferry run. If she missed it, she'd have to ask Sam to come back for her or rent a boat. And Grandmother was waiting. Her only hope was to pray that he wouldn't notice her. She couldn't face him. Or hear his voice or be forced into polite conversation.

Sam made ready at last. They began chugging their way across the water, straight into the sun, drawing a bead on the island and Sam's dock.

Thank God! Eric had not seen her. He stepped out of his car and stood near it, looking back at Charlton. Wynne kept her back to him and concentrated fiercely on the island as it grew larger and larger. She smelled the salt air and hoped that Sam would set some kind of speed record tonight. But Sam never hurried. The ferry would reach the island in its own good time.

Even with its proximity to the city of Charlton on the mainland, Feather Island had remained rather exclusive and remote. It had not yet become a true tourist haven, in the sense that other Florida areas had, and she hoped it never would. It would be spoiled then. As it was now, it was rather quaint, quiet, and offered its own way of life.

She kept thinking about such things to block out the knowledge that Eric was so near. Then she heard his footsteps behind her and gripped the railing tightly.

"Wynne?"

She gathered her courage and turned about quickly, putting a bright smile on her face, anxious to have the meeting over and done.

II

Eric gave Wynne a smile. The same dear, lopsided smile she remembered so well. His teeth flashed in his suntanned face, and even though he was dressed for his business office in Charlton, Eric had casualness written all over him.

"I knew it was you."

"So you were the late arrival," she said, as if she hadn't noticed him before. "You nearly missed the boat."

"And you're supposed to be in Tallahassee."

"I was."

"Home for a visit?" Eric asked.

"Yes. Grandmother wants to see me."

"Oh."

Everyone knew Grandmother's reputation. She was widely respected. Honored. Trusted. But perhaps not truly liked. Priscilla Russell was not the kind that welcomed people with open arms. Her reserve was difficult to penetrate, and since life on the island was of an easy nature, many simply didn't try. For some reason, Grandmother had never liked Eric, and the feeling was mutual.

He seemed to be waiting for her to say something. Why didn't he simply go away and leave her alone? But when he didn't move, she groped for a safe subject of conversation.

"How's business?" she asked politely.

"Good. If I work hard enough, I keep my head above water."

"You're being modest, I'm sure," she said. "You always—"

"Yes?"

"You always had drive," she replied and turned back

7

to the railing to watch the nose of the ferry slicing through the green water. She wished she hadn't said that. She didn't want him to think that she remembered even that much about him.

Eric leaned against the railing beside her, black hair stirring in the breeze, his green eyes under thick lashes glancing at her now and then.

"The tarpon were running last week. I didn't fare very well," he said.

"Perhaps next time."

They fell silent. She wished Sam would push the ferry a little faster. She wanted the trip over, Eric back in his car and gone.

"Perhaps you'll come with me," he said.

"What?"

"Fishing. For tarpon," he said with a searching look. She shook her head. "No. I think not."

Eric sighed. "You're still very angry with me, aren't you? After all this time. Wynne, I want to be friends. Isn't that possible?"

She felt the cool breeze on her hot face and struggled for the right words.

"No," she said quietly.

"I'm sorry for that. Truly sorry."

"Are you?"

Eric was instantly angry. "Sometimes, Wynne, you're for all the world as hard and unforgiving as your grandmother!"

She faced him, blue gray eyes flashing. Their gazes locked, and suddenly, two years had fallen away, and they were quarreling again, and everything was crashing down around her head. She struggled with all the hurt and angry words that came rising to her throat. But what good did it do to open the subject now? What good was it to remember Shelley Grant and that summer when she had come to the hotel with her parents? What good did it do to turn the knife in her heart? Shelley with her platinum hair and winsome smile, who had caught Eric's eyes so quickly, so easily! She had taken the entire matter badly then; it was painful to remember even now.

8

Eric leaned against the railing again.

"That was inexcusable of me, Wynne. I'm sorry."

"I don't want to talk about it. Now or ever. What is past is past. I believe that's what you told me."

Eric scowled. He straightened and reached up to loosen his tie. "We were both young."

"Not that young," she replied.

"Wynne—"

"Please, just leave me alone, Eric."

He ran a hand nervously through his rumpled black hair. He flushed. Then with a nod, he backed away.

"Have a nice visit," he murmured.

He left her alone at last and returned to his car. He climbed inside, and in a moment, the radio was blaring loudly, giving the evening news. She did not look back. She kept her eyes on the island. It was very near now. She could see the mangrove trees, the landing dock, and Will Dykes's garage just a short distance up the road. She watched the coconut palms swaying in the breeze and the white-winged gulls against the red sky. She kept telling herself none of the last few minutes had happened —that she had not been foolish enough to quarrel with Eric again, to let him know that she remembered anything that had happened or put any importance to it.

At last, they had reached the shore. Captain Sam made the ferry fast, and she waited until Eric and Will Dykes had driven off and disappeared down the dusty road before she stepped off herself.

"Isn't anyone meeting you, Wynne?" Captain Sam asked.

"No. They didn't know when I'd arrive," she said. "I can phone Dad."

"I'll drive you up to the hotel," Captain Sam said.

"I don't want to be a bother."

"I'll be going up to the Hurricane Haven for supper anyway. If you can wait a few minutes—"

She followed him into his little office building. There he opened the mail sack and sorted the few pieces of mail.

"You had another fight with Eric, didn't you?"

She looked up, startled. "You heard?"

"Didn't have to hear," Sam grinned. "I could almost

see that red hair of yours bristling, and I know Eric pretty well too. What did you say to him that got him so riled up?"

"Nothing."

"Ah, I see," Sam said with a wink. "Well, I never figured Eric was very smart, throwing you over for that Shelley Grant. She was a fly-by-night if I ever saw one. When the summer was over, she was gone—ain't likely she'll be back."

"Please, Sam—"

"Sorry, girl. I'm not much for tact these days. Comes from dealing with the likes of Will and some of the others on the island."

He went to turn on the dock lights so they would be burning when he came home later. He picked up her small bag and tossed it into his old Ford. They rumbled up the narrow sandy road toward the Gulf side of the island, passing Will's garage. She wondered about Lorrie, but there wasn't time to stop now. Perhaps later she would come back to pay her old friend a visit.

There were a few cottages inland, but most of them lined the shores of the island. When they reached the Gulf side, there was a cluster of buildings that made up a small business district. Here in the center of things was the South Wind Hotel. The familiar sight of it tugged at Wynne's heart. It had been home for a long time. Their apartment to the rear of the hotel had been cozy, not fancy, but serviceable, and she knew every room of the hotel as well as she knew the sight of her own face in the mirror.

Room two twenty-eight was the nicest. Those old funny porcelain faucets were in room two twenty-nine. The odd-shaped closet was in the only suite in the hotel. The rose wallpaper was in two seventeen. A dozen little things kept coming to mind as they drove past.

"Sam, remember how I used to curl up in the corner of the lobby and play my favorite game?"

Sam laughed. "People watching. I remember. You were sitting there the first time I ever saw you. I must confess it was love at first sight."

She reached out to cover his hand with hers. "Ah, Sam, you're good for a girl's ego."

"You were all eyes. Big, questioning eyes. You didn't miss a thing."

"I loved the hours I spent there. Sometimes, I read. Or listened to a little radio I had. Or I made up stories about the people staying in the hotel. I still remember that big wicker chair and how cozy my little corner was!"

"I never really thought you'd leave the island," Sam said.

"It was home," she admitted. "Deep down, I suppose it still is."

"How's your father?" Captain Sam asked.

"Fine, as far as I know."

"Hmm."

"What's that supposed to mean?"

Captain Sam shook his head. "Nothing."

"Sam, you're hiding something!"

"Don't *know* anything. Never do. I've only got hunches. Just haven't seen your father in a few days, that's all. I wondered—"

He left the sentence hanging, and a chill went through Wynne's heart. She was still shaken by her unexpected encounter with Eric, and she was not eager to face Grandmother and whatever crisis had prompted her to call Wynne home.

In a few minutes, Sam would drop her outside the house, and she would walk up the stone steps to the door and lift the heavy knocker. She would go into the meticulously kept house that smelled always of sea air and cleaning wax and join the old lady on her veranda where she had a superb view of the Gulf. Grandmother's view was surpassed perhaps only by the one enjoyed at the Hethershaw house standing on the only hill on the island a short distance away.

They had arrived. Sam stopped his car and jumped out to carry her luggage up to the door.

"Thank you, Sam. I can manage now."

"I'll be at the Hurricane if you want to join me later," Sam said.

"I'll probably not be able to get away. But before I go back to Tallahassee, I'll find time for a visit."

"You do that. Good luck, girl."

Then he was gone, waving to her, limping away to

11

his car. In a moment, he had driven out of sight, and there was only the breeze in the palms, the distant sound of the surf pounding at the shore. She lifted the knocker and let it fall.

Wilma Hinston had been with Grandmother for years. She opened the door with a welcoming smile.

"So, you've arrived! Welcome home, Wynne."

Wynne walked through the house, past a living room furnished with modern pieces, then through the dining room with its heavier and old-fashioned furniture, and on through glass doors and out to the carpeted, enclosed veranda, a large circular structure that looked toward Hethershaw's house to the north and Dolphin Bay to the south. From the west, the evening sun was pouring in. But Grandmother never complained of the heat. She liked the sun, although her only contact with it was here on the warm veranda at evening time, when she paid her respects to its dying rays.

Grandmother sat in a large wicker chair, cane grasped in one hand, wearing a prim, neat dress, pearls around her neck, her hair stylishly done and quite white now, her eyes a sharp blue as they swung toward her.

"Wynne," she said simply. "You're here."

"How are you, Grandmother?"

"Sit down. Wilma will serve us soon. You look tired."

"I am a little."

"I've inconvenienced you."

Wynne didn't reply. It hadn't been said in the nature of an apology. Grandmother seldom apologized for anything. She simply stated facts as she saw them.

"What is it? Why have you sent for me?"

"We'll eat first and then talk. Did Sam fetch you from the dock?"

"Yes."

"Have you heard from your father?"

"No. Should I have?"

Grandmother's lips made a straight line. Her knuckles showed white as she grasped the cane still tighter. Then her composure returned. She relaxed visibly, but her eyes betrayed her true feeling. Something was wrong, Grandmother was very upset, and it had to do with Dad!

Wilma came to lay the table. She brought out several

dishes, served them, and then discreetly disappeared. Grandmother poured the hot tea. She seldom drank anything cold. The casserole was tasty, the biscuits hot and flaky, the jam some that Wilma had put up herself.

But Wynne had trouble eating or enjoying any of the food. Her appetite was about to drown itself in unasked questions. How could Grandmother sit there so calmly, as if nothing had happened, as if this was like any normal day?

Now and then, Grandmother paused in eating to glance out at the Gulf. Fishermen from Charlton were coming in from their day's work. An occasional pleasure craft went skimming the water. The Hethershaw sails were white and lovely against the sky as they drifted to shore.

Dessert was fresh fruit, another cup of tea, and a move from the table to the wicker chairs facing the water.

"Now," Grandmother said.

Wynne braced herself.

III

ERIC CHANNON KNEW Wynne was waiting for him to
leave the ferry before she would go herself, so he drove
off rapidly. As a gentleman, he wanted to offer her a
ride home. But under the circumstances, it didn't seem
wise. Wynne would have refused him anyway. She
wanted nothing to do with him, even in the most casual
of ways. It was there in the tone of her voice and in the
very way she had stood as they talked, almost haughty,
shoulders rigid, head up, chin out. Like Grandmother
Priscilla. For all the world! It was just that Wynne was
taller, younger, more beautiful than Priscilla Russell had
ever been, even in her heyday.

"Why?" he asked aloud. "Why has she come back?"

Perhaps there was some family emergency. Who could
tell? With Priscilla Russell at the head of that family, it
could be anything. Priscilla was not one of his favorite
people. Wynne's father was nice enough. But why the
man had let his mother dominate him for fifteen years
while he operated the hotel was beyond Eric. Everyone
on the island knew that while Harvey Russell sat at the
front desk, it was the old lady behind the scenes who
really ran things. But he'd been unkind in comparing
Wynne with her grandmother. Wynne was fresh, pleasant, trusting, vulnerable. Perhaps too vulnerable. That
was why she had been hurt so badly when he—

He turned his thoughts away. Why think of that
now? The door was closed, the key turned, the chain in
place. He was locked out forever.

Eric reached his house in a scorching ten minutes,
three minutes under his average time. He slammed the
car door loudly, as if to drown out the sound of the surf,
which for some reason ground at his nerves tonight.

He lived alone. Once a week a woman came in, cleaned, saw to his laundry, and then left him alone. It was the way he wanted it.

The phone rang. For a crazy moment, he thought it might be Wynne.

"Eric? Delmer Whitlow. Coming tonight?"

Eric licked his lips. "I'm not sure I can make it, Delmer, I have a date."

"It's important. We've called the meeting for seven-thirty. Won't keep you long."

Eric ran a hand over his forehead and felt the beads of perspiration there. How had he gotten into this anyway? Why couldn't he gracefully bow out? But then, he knew why. He was already involved. The committee wasn't going to let him forget it.

"I'll do my best, Delmer."

"Fine. Seven-thirty. My place."

They hung up. Eric took a deep breath. He had no intention of seeing Karen tonight. But often, he took his boat and buzzed over to the mainland. A call from the dock and Karen would come in her car to pick him up. They would spend the hours parked under a palm tree just talking, or eating a sandwich somewhere. A very simple arrangement. Karen didn't demand much. No fancy expensive dates. Just as long as they were together. She was an unbelievably sweet girl. No temper tantrums. No jealousy. Just a nice girl with brown hair and blue eyes who thought the sun rose and set in him. What more could a man want?

A tantalizing smile that played havoc with a man's nerves? Blue gray eyes as changeable as the sea? Hair the color of russet leaves in the fall or burnished mahogany? A tall, lovely woman more mature than Karen would ever be?

Eric jerked at his tie with a ruthless motion. Why was he thinking about Wynne like this? It was over and done between them. She had not forgotten, nor had she forgiven the things he had done. The stupid, foolish, wasteful, fanciful things!

The phone rang again. He answered it gruffly.

"Hey, what's wrong?" Karen laughed. "You sound so grouchy."

15

"Sorry. How are you, Karen?"

"Lonely. Why don't you come over and take me for a long ride in your boat? The bay's very calm. It's going to be a lovely night. I just know it."

He smiled. She was so easy to please. So agreeable. So eager to show him that she loved him.

"I have to come back for a meeting. If there's time afterwards, I'll phone. OK?"

"Oh, good! I'll be waiting. Bye darling."

In the kitchen, he made a thick sandwich, opened a bottle of milk, poured a tall glass, and carried it all to his patio where he could look out over the ocean and see the curve of Dolphin Bay. Wynne used to run there, barefoot, red hair flying, daring him to give chase, daring him even more to catch up and sweep her into his arms. They were happy then, young. What had happened?

Eric lit a cigarette and knew what had happened. Shelley Grant had happened. Shelly with her platinum blonde hair, her blue eyes, her slender figure, her slight Southern drawl, and her witch's ways! She'd come to Feather Island to spend the summer with her parents, who had been there before. But it was the first time for Shelley. Always before she had been going to college or touring Europe or simply doing as she pleased elsewhere.

Shelley had built a fire inside his heart that was awesome with its intensity. He'd lost reason, good sense, and more important than anything he'd lost Wynne. It served him right. But he hated it that Wynne disliked him so now.

He bit savagely into his sandwich. Then there was the problem of tonight's meeting. He wished he didn't belong to the committee. He felt like a Judas.

He finished eating, drained his glass, and looked at his watch. There was time to shower and change. An hour later, he went down to his dock, checked the boat and shoved off.

The committee was made up of twelve businessmen in Charlton. Delmer was its head. The conference room was blue with cigar smoke.

"Come in, Eric," Delmer said heartily. "I want you to meet the senator. He's got good news for us tonight."

"The allocations have been approved?"

Delmer gave him a hearty wink. "A survey team will be in the area very soon. We're going to get that bridge!"

"I see."

Delmer laughed. "Sound a little happier, man. The bridge will bring more people, more tourists, more business. We all know that! Charlton will boom. It will put cash in our pockets. And think about Feather Island. You're lucky, man. You already own a piece of it."

Eric's stomach did a strange flip-flop. His was a divided soul. Charlton needed the bridge to Feather Island for the revenue it would bring in one way or another. The island *didn't* need the bridge because it would spoil what was now almost a Garden of Eden. He loved the island as it was. But of course he saw its great possibilities too.

"I've got a development company interested," Delmer said. "On the q.t., of course. We have to keep this quiet. You know how most of those people are over on the island."

"They're not going to like it," Eric said with a sigh. "Most of them hate the idea—they're an exclusive lot."

Delmer laughed. "Wait until they see the color of the money that will come pouring in. That will change their minds in a hurry."

But Eric wondered. He thought of Max Hethershaw, that strange, remote man who had lived for years on the island. No one really knew him. Everyone knew his new wife, Ilsa, but no one knew Max. Max liked it that way. Then there were countless others. Friendly, nice. With each other. But not with strangers. They would loathe being commercialized.

The meeting was a short one as Delmer had promised. The senator made a nice speech which was interrupted often with rounds of applause and cheers of elation. Eric only half heard.

"Now, gentlemen, please understand that this is merely in the speculation stage. Approval will have to come down from the capital," the senator was saying. "But as soon

17

as the surveys are completed and estimates made for total cost, it will only be a matter of time before it is all put into operation."

At last, the meeting adjourned. Eric stepped outside to the fresh air and made for the nearest telephone booth.

Karen's car was a modest one, and she drove it with care. A few minutes later, she pulled alongside him, and he jumped in.

"Where are we off to?" Karen asked.

"You wanted a boat ride."

"Only if you want to go. You sound depressed, darling."

"It's politics. About the bridge."

Thank God, no one on Feather Island knew he belonged to that committee. It had been one of the stipulations he'd made when he joined them. He had to live over there with those people, and when they heard, they'd hate him.

"Don't look so serious, darling. Give me a kiss," Karen said.

He leaned over and kissed her cheek. She drove down toward the dock. A few minutes later, they were in the boat, and he sent it skimming the water of the bay, running lights burning, watching the lighted markers he knew so well. He circled one of them, and Karen laughed. Then he cut the motor and let them drift. He kissed her once, twice, several times. There was something unique about being in a boat out in the middle of the sound with the stars shining and a fair breeze blowing. But his heart wasn't with it, and soon he made an excuse and headed back to shore.

There, he told Karen good-night. She insisted she could drive home alone. He knew she was still on the shore watching him as he headed his boat back toward Feather Island.

He rounded the far end and approached Dolphin Bay. He barely saw the other boat in time. With a sharp spin of the wheel, he narrowly avoided a collision.

"Hey! Your lights are out! What are you doing?"

Of course he couldn't be heard over the roar of the motor. What fathead was anchored out there at this time of night without a light showing? He knew the boat. It was called the *Lazy Day*, a rental from Charlton. But who was aboard or why they were there, he had no idea.

Reaching home, he hurried up to his house from the dock and let himself in. Remembering the boat and still angry, he went to the patio with a pair of binoculars. It was hard seeing in the dark, but with a careful sweep of the glasses, he was certain the bay was now empty. The boat had gone

He slept poorly that night. Then, the next morning, he ate breakfast at the Hurricane Haven before catching Sam's seven-thirty ferry for Charlton. When he was halfway through eating, he glanced out the window. The beach in front of the South Wind Hotel was directly in his line of vision. He saw a young man, blond, tall, suntanned, struggling with a mountain of luggage.

Then looking beyond him, Eric saw the boat. The *Lazy Day*.

IV

An insect hit against the screen wire of the veranda. Grandmother leaned forward in her chair, and Wynne was conscious of holding her breath, afraid to speculate, worried about what she was to hear.

"You're to take over the hotel," Grandmother said.

For a moment, Wynne couldn't believe she had heard correctly.

"But what about Dad?"

"I never want to hear his name mentioned again. Do you understand? Never!"

Wynne's heart was racing. Grandmother and Dad often quarreled. Usually about small things. But obviously this was different.

"I expect you'll have some ideas," Grandmother was saying. "I'll listen to them. You're young and smart. You're my granddaughter. You can handle it, Wynne."

"But Grandmother—"

"The South Wind is a clean, sensible, nice hotel. The way people want it. We're unique, like Feather Island itself. A different cup of tea. You remember that, Wynne."

"I want to know what happened. Surely I am entitled to an explanation!"

Grandmother ignored the request. Silence grew for a moment on the veranda, broken only by the slushing of the surf over the sand.

"If you won't tell me what's going on, I'll speak with Dad."

Still Grandmother didn't say a word or move.

"All right then. I'll go see him now—"

Grandmother didn't turn her head as Wynne got to her feet and quickly walked through the house to the door. It was dusk. She walked along the familiar street, her head in a spin. The last thing in the world she wanted to do was come back to the island permanently. For all its loveliness, she didn't want to stay.

The breakers were crashing against the shore. The sky was flushed with the last of the sunset, and she tried not to notice how beautiful it was or to remember that only hours ago she'd been experiencing homesick pangs.

The South Wind faced the Gulf, a two-story building, painted white and trimmed in green. It was only a small hotel with ten rooms and one large suite on the second floor. On the ground floor there was a large lobby, a small office, and the apartment where she had lived with her parents. Now that Mother was dead, her father lived there alone. About three months ago, he had brought in an assistant, Edward Allen, who lived in one of the rooms to the rear, rent free, as part of his salary.

Wynne heard a car coming down the road, very fast, and for a moment, she feared it was going to be Eric. She couldn't endure still another encounter with him. Hadn't the first one been enough?

But she saw that the red sports car belonged to Ilsa Hethershaw. Wynne caught a glimpse of her mane of black hair flying in the breeze. Somewhere about her person there was sure to be a bright scarf and a heavy scent of perfume. Those were Ilsa's trademarks.

"She's not like anyone else on the island," Grandmother had always said. "She doesn't belong here. Max was wrong to bring her."

"She's very young and very pretty."

"Too young for Max Hethershaw," Grandmother pointed out. "She'll never stay."

"But rumors have it that Hethershaw is mad for her," Wynne said.

"Hmmph," Grandmother replied. "It's his third time around. There's no fool like an old fool."

That had ended the conversation. But Ilsa Hethershaw, a resident now for the past year, was the source of most talk on the island. Hethershaw himself was often a target of gossip. He was a man of wealth. He had banking interests on the mainland, owned the biggest house on the island, and lived up to his image. But he didn't mix. He was aloof to the rest of the island people. Many didn't like him for that reason, although still, many envied him. If they disliked him, they hated him vigorously. A man of controversy. But how had he managed to capture a girl like Ilsa? No one seemed to have the answer to that one. Unless it was the smell of money.

The walk from her grandmother's house to the hotel took about ten minutes. The South Wind looked cozy in the twilight. Lights burned in the lobby, but Wynne went around to the side entrance and rapped at the door of the apartment. She tried the door, and it came open.

"Dad? Are you here? I'm home."

For a moment, she saw or heard nothing, and she had a terrible feeling that he had already gone. Then a lighter flashed on, and she saw her father sitting by the window, putting the flame to a fresh cigar.

"I was expecting you. Come in, Wynne."

"Why are you sitting in the dark?" she asked with a light voice. She reached out and turned on the lamp. Dad blinked in the sudden brightness, and she got another shock. He looked so haggard. His eyes were red as if he hadn't slept well for several nights.

"I suppose she phoned you," he said bitterly.

"What's happened? She hasn't told me anything."

"We had a fight to end all fights. It comes down to one simple fact. Priscilla won't change. . . .

". . . and I wanted to make changes. She wouldn't hear of it. The hotel is old, Wynne. It grows more shabby and obsolete every year."

"I still don't understand! You're talking in circles, Dad."

"All right. In a word, it's the bridge."

"The bridge!"

"It's going to come. Any fool knows it will. When it does, people will come. The island will change. There will be new business, new hotels, motels, cottages. Fancy new places. Do you think for a minute that the South Wind will be able to compete with that?"

She was startled and a little shocked.

"Dad, are you *for* the bridge?"

"Does it matter? Don't you see, Wynne, the South Wind can't survive as it is now. It's on its last legs, and Priscilla won't admit it. She won't see it. She won't let go."

"She's not alone in hating the idea of the bridge," Wynne pointed out. "The island is perfect as it is. The bridge will spoil it!"

Dad took a deep breath. "I see. So, you're siding with her."

"I'm not siding with anyone. I just don't want you to go, Dad."

"I've saved a little nest egg. I intend to travel. See the country. Then when I'm tired of that, I'll settle in some place like an old pelican and watch the sunsets."

He went into the bedrooom and came back with two pieces of luggage.

"I've arranged for someone to take me over to Charlton. I'm late."

"Oh, Dad!"

He put a hand on her shoulder. When Wynne's mother died, Wynne had hoped that they would grow closer, but it hadn't worked that way. They had a true fondness for each other, but they had never been able to confide in one another. They had shared no secrets. Her father had inherited his reserve from Priscilla whether he liked to admit it or not.

"Wynne, I've never told you what to do. I've given you a free rein. This time, I'm going to break the rule. Don't stay here. Don't let your grandmother hold you against your will. If you do, you're a fool!"

Then he bent down and kissed her cheek. In a moment, he had gone. When the door had closed behind him the room seemed very empty and lonely.

In a little while, she went back outside and walked toward the beach. Her emotions were in a whirl. Dad was for the bridge. Dad was for changing the island. The bridge was a hotly discussed subject. Most were against it. Only a few were trying hard to make it a reality. She knew how Grandmother felt. It tore at Wynne's heart to think of the South Wind unable to support itself, to be lost in the change and the glitter of the tourist world.

23

She stared at the sea, perhaps for answers to all the questions in her heart. The last of the red sky was gone. The surf rolled in, foaming white on the sand. The sandpipers were strutting and darting along the edge of the water, picking in the sand with their beaks. The last of the beachcombers were strolling along lazily, going home.

She tried to think of Tallahassee and her work there. She told herself she would be faced with constant encounters with Eric if she stayed. How could she endure that?

She knew Grandmother was waiting. But she couldn't go back just yet. There was so much to consider. Perhaps Dad was right about the whole business. But on the other hand—she turned to look back at the old hotel, and her heart went out to it. She loved it. She truly did.

Next door, she saw the swinging signboard of the Hurricane Haven. It served as the main restaurant on the island and was the only place open at night. It was owned by Ruby Hammer. Brash, likable, widowed Ruby. Everyone's friend. More than a year ago, Dad had closed the coffee shop in the South Wind and sent their patrons to Ruby. Ruby was glad for the extra business, and it solved a headache which had been growing in the hotel for some time.

Wynne went toward the Hurricane with mixed emotions. She had come here so often with Eric.

Inside, the motif was bamboo. Hurricane lamps. Fishing nets. Shells. Intimate booths, well-placed tables. It never changed.

"Wynne!"

Ruby Hammer came toward her, a large woman with gray-streaked brown hair done in a bun at the nape of her neck, dark eyes flashing, her smile as big as the outdoors. Wynne found herself being hugged heartily, and it was like being surrounded by a soft feather bed.

"It's so good to see you, Wynne!" Ruby said. "How's Tallahassee? How long will you stay?"

"A day or so," she replied cautiously. "Is Captain Sam still here?"

"Over there in his favorite booth."

Captain Sam jumped to his feet as she sat down

24

opposite him. A small deck of playing cards was spread out on the table, and he'd been having a game of solitaire.

"Who won?" she asked.

"Me," he said with a grin.

"You cheated."

"Not a chance!" he retorted. "Have you been next door?"

She took a deep breath. "Yes. You know about Dad, don't you?"

"Just the talk. Is he really leaving?"

"He's gone. A few minutes ago."

"So what happens now?"

"I don't know, Sam. And that's the truth."

She tried to put it all out of her mind as she watched Sam play another game. A few customers came in. A few went out. The rush hour was over. The island was settling down for a night of peace. Darkness was falling deeply outside the window. It was so quiet here. A green garden in the arms of the green sea.

"Sam, what shall I do?"

Sam's blue eyes searched hers for a moment. "What your heart tells you, I suppose."

"I'm so confused. So torn."

Captain Sam reached out to pat her hand. "Whatever you do, girl, I know it will be the right thing."

"Thanks for the vote of confidence," she laughed. "Now, I must get back. Grandmother isn't the most patient person in the world."

"I'll drive you."

"Thanks, but I'll walk. I need the time to think."

She was tempted to go by and see Lorrie, but it was some distance to Lorrie's house from the Hurricane, and the sooner she settled things with Grandmother the better.

She reached the house a short time later. As she expected, Grandmother was still on the veranda. It looked as if she hadn't moved since she had left her.

"Dad's gone," Wynne said.

Grandmother's lip made a straight line, but she made no reply.

"Grandmother, I'm *not* a hotel manager!" Wynne burst out.

"Are you saying no without even giving it a chance?

25

Do you want me to sell the hotel? Do you want the South Wind in the hands of strangers?"

"You speak of it as if it were more than boards and plaster and glass!"

"Isn't it?" Grandmother asked quietly.

Wynne tried to speak, to find some logical answer to that and found there was none. The South Wind was theirs. It always had been.

Grandmother nodded. "You'll stay."

Wynne felt herself being swept into a kind of eddy, swirling around and around. She was being trapped. Captured in some fine silken web she couldn't see.

"I'd rather not," she replied quickly. "For many reasons. None of them because I don't love the South Wind. You have to believe that, Grandmother."

Grandmother got to her feet. Her small stature always came as a shock to Wynne. She was a woman with a great deal of influence and power. A woman with strength. And yet, all of this was caged in a small, frail body barely five feet tall.

"It's because of Eric, I suppose."

Wynne blinked and drew a deep breath with sharp surprise.

"It's time you cope with that, Wynne. Past time. How better than to stay here and face the music? It never helps to run."

Grandmother's understanding of how she felt came as a total surprise. Was there no end to the old woman's perception?

"He's engaged now, you know," Grandmother said. "Some girl over on the mainland."

Wynne closed her eyes, a harsh ache cutting her heart. "All the more reason not to stay," she murmured.

"Nonsense! We Russells don't run. We stay, and we look everybody in the eye without shame or pity. We don't give in to weakness. We are as strong as we want to be. Stronger!"

Wynne twisted her hands together. "You perhaps. Not me."

There was an awkward silence. Grandmother sat down again, and she seemed very small and alone. She always looked a person straight in the eye when she talked with them, but now, she dropped her gaze. Her hand was trembling as she gripped her cane.

"Wynne, child, I need you."

The words caught Wynne totally unprepared. She had never heard Grandmother say that to any one before. But it was there, in a quiet, thoughtful, longing voice, and Wynne suddenly felt very young, very tender. She loved this old lady with a special kind of love that was a secret warmth inside her. Grandmother was unique. Steel overlaid with lace. And yet here was Grandmother, the strong one who now suddenly seemed the weaker. Wynne knew that she was caught and held by some silver thread that stretched between them. Call it family bonds or call it love or just the will and strength of the older passing to the younger. Whatever it was, Wynne knew she was licked.

She reached out and touched Grandmother's small hand and felt it stop trembling beneath her fingers.

"All right, Grandmother. I'll stay."

V

WYNNE SPENT THE NIGHT in the guest room at her grandmother's house. She slept very little, wondering how she had committed herself so easily and so quickly. But it was done now.

Over breakfast, Grandmother seemed calm, almost happy.

"You must speak with Edward Allen," she said. "Tell him of the changes."

"I'll have to go back to Tallahassee for a few days," Wynne pointed out. "So I'll go down to the South Wind this morning and see if there are any immediate problems."

Wynne left the house shortly after breakfast and walked to the hotel. Grandmother had a car, a rather old one, which she no longer drove. It was up to Wilma to act as chauffeur if the occasion arose. But Wynne would bring her own car back from Tallahassee and move back into the hotel. She thought about Jack Brown and about her work in Tallahassee and all the ideas she had that would now go to waste. Had she let her sentiment rule her good sense?

In the broad light of day, the hotel showed signs of wear. It needed fresh paint. The salt air had taken its toll in many ways, and while it had withstood a number of hurricanes in its time, it probably couldn't endure many more.

"Wynne! Hello!"

She looked around at the shout and saw an elderly man waving to her. George Laughlin. He was a permanent resident in the hotel, room two twenty. He was retired, had little family, and loafed away the days, walking the beach, occasionally going fishing, and in general, doing as little as possible. He came to shake Wynne's hand, his bald head shining in the sun. He always made her think of a scrubbed cherub.

"Is it true your father has gone?" George asked. "I knocked on his door this morning, and there was no answer."

"Yes. He's gone, George. You're looking at the new manager."

George's brows went up. "Well, well! I should have guessed."

"I must go and speak with Edward. If you'll excuse me—"

"Now, look at that!" George said with an air of disgust. "Looks like they could act their age. Nettie, in particular!"

He was referring to two more of their guests. They spent every summer on Feather Island, arriving the last of May and staying until October, occupying the only suite in the hotel. They were twins and in their seventies. Nettie was the stronger of the two. Lettie always took Nettie's lead. Right now, they looked like beachcombers, with straw hats, shorts showing their knobby knees and legs no longer pretty, each toting a plastic pail over her arm.

"They've collected enough shells in their time to pave a street from here to Rome!" George complained.

"I see you and the Wilkin twins are still great friends," Wynne teased.

"Lettie wouldn't be so bad if she had a chance," George muttered. "But that Nettie—now I ask you, don't they look ridiculous?"

It wasn't exactly the word for it. Their beach wear did little to enhance their beauty, but on the island, casualness was the keynote in everything.

Wynne waved to the twins before she crossed the old-fashioned front veranda with its assortment of chairs and went into the lobby. She paused for a moment. There were two small potted palms, a rubber plant, several divans and chairs. The old Persian rug with its floral design was showing worn spots. The desk was curved, and immediately behind it was the pigeonholed cabinet holding the room keys and the mail for the guests.

The wide, carpeted stairs led up to the rooms above. The old coffee table held magazines. There was a rack of colorful folders and information about the island. Bamboo awnings were rolled high at the windows and letting in the first of the morning sunlight.

She sent a quick glance to her special corner, smiling to herself. Oh, to be so young again, so eager, so wrapped up in a child's world where everything and everyone in it seemed very dear and very special!

"Hello, Edward."

Edward Allen looked up from his desk with a start. Was he as surprised to see her as he seemed? Or had Dad prepared him for her possible arrival?

"Have you got time for a chat?" Wynne asked, walking into the office. He followed her. Dad's desk was piled untidily with papers. She sat down behind it. Edward paused, a tall, impeccably dressed man who always looked pale.

"I'm taking over the hotel, Edward."

He licked his lips. "I see." Had he hoped to become the new manager himself?

"How many rooms are occupied?"

"One room and the suite the Wilkin women always rent."

"Is that all?"

"The summer's young, and these months are usually slow."

"That's true," Wynne said. "Well, I guess I'd better see the ledgers, any unpaid bills, and any other business that needs attention."

"Yes, right away."

"Are there any reservations?"

"The Grants are coming. I understand they're old customers."

Wynne gripped the edge of the desk. She didn't like remembering the Grants.

"Two or three people?" she asked quickly.

"Just two."

She was relieved. Then Shelley wasn't coming. Thank God for that!

"Then there is a Diane Carlson who wants a room for the entire summer," Edward said. "She requested a room with a view of the Gulf. I gave her two twenty-six."

Edward brought the ledgers and a few file folders. It looked as if it was going to be a long morning.

"Edward, would you mind going next door and bringing some coffee?"

It wasn't that she needed or really wanted the coffee. Perhaps it was that she wanted to be alone here for a few minutes. She leaned back in her father's chair and looked at the little, familiar office. It needed fresh paint. New furnishings. New carpeting. But then, she knew that the entire hotel needed freshening.

"Oh, what am I doing here?" she asked herself. "Why have I agreed to stay?"

In a few minutes, she heard Edward coming back. She took a deep breath and began going through the ledgers. At least they were still solvent. There were only a few unpaid bills. But to make any kind of profit at all, they needed more guests. She heard the bell at the front desk, and leaving Edward to add a column of figures for her, she went to see who was there so early in the morning.

"Hello," the man said with a quick nod.

He was tall, blond and blue-eyed with a nice smile. A total stranger.

"Any chance for a room?"

"Ocean view?" Wynne asked.

"I'd like that."

"Would you sign the register, please? How long will you be staying?"

He gave her a quick look. "Probably most of the summer."

He scrawled his name and address. He was from North Dakota. Brad Sherman.

"A long way from home," she said with a smile. "But welcome to the South Wind, Mr. Sherman. I'll give you room two twenty-eight. It's the largest and has a very good view."

31

"Thank you. One other thing. I've chartered a boat for the summer. Will it be all right to tie it up at your dock?"

"Of course. But we do charge two dollars a day for that."

"I've a great deal of diving gear on board. I don't especially like leaving it there. Would you have any place I could store it?"

"We've a supply room to the rear of the hotel. If that would do."

"Good!"

He gave her another attractive smile. She was more than a little curious about how he had happened to come here.

There was the business of paying for the room—a week in advance was always requested—giving him the key, and showing him the room. It was plain, simply furnished, but one of the better ones in the hotel. The view was superb. From the second-story window, they could see far to the horizon, and the sky was clear and unblemished without a cloud in sight. Only a tanker far in the distance could be seen on the aquamarine water.

Beside her, Brad Sherman drew a deep breath. "I'd heard this was a beautiful spot!"

Wynne spent the rest of the morning putting order to the office, rechecking the books, and wondering what she could do to bolster business. The McCalls, Pete and Marge, handled most of the work around the hotel. Pete took care of repairs and the grounds, while Marge looked after the rooms. When they arrived for work, Wynne called them into her office.

"You're back, Miss Russell," Marge said with a happy smile. "I knew you'd come."

"How did you know that?"

"We know your grandmother," Pete said with a grin.

"I'll have some things I'll want done. Pete, I wish you'd make an estimate as to how much it would cost to give the hotel a fresh coat of paint."

"Will do, Miss Russell."

"And you, Marge, if there are things that need to be done in any of the rooms, make a list, will you?"

32

Marge nodded. "All right. But I'm warning you. It will be a long one!"

At lunch time, Wynne went next door to the Hurricane Haven. Sam was there, as were a few of the islanders, and the twins, Nettie and Lettie, who immediately put their heads together when they saw her. Wynne knew they were talking about her managing the hotel. Gossip was something they thrived on. But all in all, they were good old souls, and they had been coming to the South Wind every summer for years.

Ruby gave her a bright grin, and Wynne knew that Edward had spread the word about her staying.

"Glad to have you back, Wynne. You belong here," Ruby said. "Say, who's the stranger?"

Brad Sherman was coming in the door. He was so tall his head nearly touched the top of the doorsill. He paused, looking around. Then he saw Wynne and smiled. He came straight toward her table.

"Hello, Miss Russell. Would you mind if I joined you?"

"Of course not."

Brad folded his long legs under the table and began to study the menu. "What's good?" he asked.

He was very attractive. Everything from the curly blond hair to the sun-bronzed skin to the blue eyes with their silver specks.

"I recommend the special. You never go wrong with that."

He smiled. "Then I'll try it. Do you ever go diving, Miss Russell?"

"No."

"What a pity! There's nothing like it."

"You seem to have enough enthusiasm for everyone. You're from North Dakota. An inland state. How did you get interested in diving?"

"I didn't always live there. I've been diving ever since I was a kid. There's nothing like it. I can hardly wait to get into that blue water."

"You sound enchanted already."

"I teach school, Miss Russell. I endure all those long classroom hours by thinking ahead to the summer, clear skies, deep water, and enough air to keep me down for as long as I like!"

"Can't it be a dangerous hobby?"

"Sometimes," he nodded. "It doesn't bother me. But I'll need someone from time to time to go out with me. I never make a deep dive without someone topside. Do you know of some young boy, a teenager, who would be reliable and interested in working for me?"

Lorrie's young brother, Johnny, would be just perfect for the job, Wynne decided. "He's fourteen, reliable," she told Sherman. "I'm sure he'd be happy to have the job. I'll get in touch with him and have him come around to see you."

"I'd appreciate that very much. . . . Tell me, have you always lived on Feather Island?"

"For years."

"Anything I should know about it?"

She smiled. "Only that when a hurricane blows in, run for cover."

"What about the water?"

"Mangrove Sound is normally quiet. Of course, the Gulf is different."

"And the bay to the south?"

"Dolphin Bay? Safe. Little undertow. But Egret Bay to the north is another matter. The water just below the cliff is very deep and dangerous. Don't let a high tide catch you there or you could be in trouble."

"What about sharks?"

"They've been sighted occasionally. Not often. Some say the porpoise keep them away."

"Does anyone ever go diving around here?" he asked.

It seemed a casual question. Yet, somehow, she didn't think it was.

"A few once in a while, but not often."

"It's another world down there, Miss Russell. Perhaps someday, you'll let me show it to you."

She shook her head. "No. Thank you. I like to keep my feet on the ground."

The twins, Nettie and Lettie, were taking this all in. They were wondering who this handsome stranger was and why he was talking so earnestly with Wynne. The two old ladies would have some wild speculation going

34

in no time. Next to beach walking, other people's romance was their chief amusement.

Brad Sherman looked across the table to her, and something in his blue eyes held her.

"I'll make a wager with you, Miss Russell. I'll make a believer out of you. Before the summer's over, you'll make a dive with me."

VI

WYNNE KNEW she was expected to stay with Grandmother and take the evening meal with her until she moved into the hotel. It was nearly five o'clock when she left the South Wind. Where had the day gone? She had tried to reach Lorrie by phone several times during the afternoon, but there was no answer.

Grandmother was waiting for her on the veranda, and soon Wilma served them a refreshing meal. Grandmother asked but a few cautious questions, and Wynne sensed that the old lady was afraid she would change her mind and go back to Tallahassee. But Wynne had given her word, and she would honor it.

"I'd like to visit Lorrie this evening, Grandmother," she said.

"You may take the car if you want."

"Thank you," Wynne shook her head. "But I believe I'll walk. The hike will do me good."

"When I was young, I liked to walk too." Grandmother smiled. "Shank's mare is still the best kind."

Wynne left the house and enjoyed the twilight as she walked the familiar streets and then down the road that connected the Gulf side of the island to the bay side. There was a light in Captain Sam's office, but he was not there. She paused for a moment to look across the water to Charlton. The green street lights were strung out like baubles on a string. She walked on. Will Dykes's garage was dark. But a light burned in the house nearby, and with quick anticipation, she hurried the rest of the way, suddenly eager to see her oldest and dearest friend.

Will answered her knock, bony shoulders poking up against his blue work shirt, a toothpick in his mouth. His sparse hair looked as if it hadn't been combed since

36

morning, and he badly needed a shave. The Dyke home was a modest one, and Lorrie had done the best she could with it. Her mother had been dead for many years. It had fallen to Lorrie to hold the family together.

"Wynne!" Lorrie called. "Is that you?"

Lorrie came out of the kitchen, untying an apron. She was a tiny woman, with large brown eyes and silken blond hair. But she had changed. There was a harsh line between her brows, and the softness of a pretty mouth had disappeared.

"Lorrie!"

Wynne reached out to give her a quick, impulsive hug, and for a moment, it seemed Lorrie shrank away.

"I'd heard you were back," Lorrie said. "It's great to see you."

Then why the restraint, why the lack of warmth? Something was wrong here, and she had no idea what.

Young Johnny came to the kitchen door to nod to her with a shy smile. He was growing fast, a likable, gentle boy as Lorrie had once been gentle. It was their father, Will, that somehow didn't seem to belong here. Will Dykes was another matter altogether. He'd always been strict with his children, a penny pincher and a man who played all the angles and always in the favor of Will Dykes, the devil hang the rest.

She decided to tell Lorrie later about the job for Johnny and let her handle it. Somehow, she was always reluctant to talk about anything in front of Will Dykes.

"Could we go for a walk, Lorrie?" Wynne asked.

"Love to!" Lorrie replied.

They left the house, and as they had many times in the past, they moved northward along the beach. It was not as picturesque on the bay side of the island. But it was pleasant, and they had come this way so often that they knew every rock, every tree, every knoll, and every spot where they could pause to rest and talk in comfort.

"I heard you were going to take over the hotel," Lorrie said.

"Surprised?"

"In a way. I think you're a fool to want to come back here!"

"Lorrie!"

"I was never anything but honest with you, was I?" Lorrie asked.

"No."

"Oh, don't pay any attention to me. You know how it is. I'm aching to get off the island, and here you've had your chance and are coming back!"

"I felt I must," Wynne said. "I'm not sure I can explain it. Something about Grandmother—"

"You're a sentimentalist," Lorrie sighed. "You always were. Well, I wish you luck. I think you're going to have a real job on your hands."

"You know me. I was never afraid of a challenge," Wynne replied. "By the way, I have a job for Johnny if he's interested. A man checked into the hotel today. He wants to do some diving this summer, and he needs someone in the boat to help him. Would Johnny—"

"That sounds wonderful! It would be a relief to know he's got something to keep him busy. He's just at the age where—well, you know. Young boys get into trouble so easily."

Wynne frowned. "You shouldn't have to worry about Johnny like this, Lorrie."

Lorrie laughed shortly. "You know I do. Until he's full-grown and on his own. Dad—well, you know how it is with Dad."

"Why do you stay? Why, Lorrie?"

"I just told you. Johnny. I can't desert him, not yet."

"I suppose not."

"Listen to me, will you? I guess I'm just as much a softie as you are."

Wynne laughed. "I've got a wonderful idea. I have to go back to Tallahassee. Why don't you come with me? We'll have a kind of holiday together. Something we've never had."

Lorrie was quiet for a moment. "It's sweet of you to think of me. I'd love to go."

"Then it's settled!"

"But I can't," Lorrie said quickly. "I'm working at the big house on the cliff."

Wynne came to a dead halt. "You're working for the Hethershaws?" she asked with surprise. "Doing what?"

"They gave it a fancy name. Social secretary. You

38

know I took that business correspondence course. I take care of Ilsa's mail, run errands for her, help her keep her wardrobe in tip-top shape, and I type a few letters for Max. Business things."

"I see."

"Dad arranged it. Anything with a motor up there Dad keeps going. I still don't really know how he managed to swing the job for me, but he did."

"I'm surprised. About the whole arrangement."

Lorrie seemed very quiet, rather withdrawn, and Wynne sensed that she didn't want to talk about the Hethershaws anymore.

"Are you really going to be happy here, Wynne?" Lorrie asked.

Wynne looked out to the rippling water of Mangrove Sound as it glinted in the starlight.

"Would you believe I don't know?"

"Because of Eric?"

Wynne's heart gave a wrench. "I don't know that either. I saw him last night. On the five o'clock ferry. My luck."

"He's as handsome as ever."

"And engaged I hear."

"Yes. But he never was right for you, Wynne. I never truly thought so."

They walked on. In the darkness, it seemed to Wynne that Lorrie's voice sounded tired, strained. Was working for the Hethershaws so hard? Or was there more? Lorrie had always been a sunny, laughing, happy kind of girl. Despite her problems on the home front, she enjoyed life. She was fun to be around, but tonight, Wynne sensed that her old friend had changed.

They walked for nearly an hour before Wynne decided she should get back to the hotel.

"I'll drive you," Lorrie said. "If you don't mind riding in the truck. Dad just won't keep a decent car for us to use."

"The truck will be fine. In fact, it takes me back. Remember how we used to drive all over the island in it? What fun we had!"

"I remember," Lorrie said, and her voice sounded sad. They returned to the house and climbed into the old truck. It was noisy and smelled of gasoline fumes. They bumped and jiggled all the way back to the main road and then to the South Wind. Was that Ilsa Hethershaw's car parked there?

"It's great seeing you again, Lorrie. When I get back from Tallahassee, we'll plan something. We'll have fun this summer, like we used to."

Suddenly, Lorrie's hand was gripping Wynne's arm in a tight, frightened grasp. Her fingers were ice-cold.

"Wynne—"

"Yes. What is it, Lorrie? What's wrong?"

Then Lorrie took her hand away with a shake of her head. "Nothing."

"But you were going to say something. What was it?"

"Forget it. Please. Good-night, Wynne."

Wynne climbed out of the old truck, puzzled, curious, and a little anxious. Lorrie had not been herself all evening.

Edward was perched behind the desk. He got nervously to his feet when she came in. Wynne paused for a moment. She noticed the scent of perfume, very heavy, drifting on the air. The kind of perfume Ilsa Hethershaw always drowned herself in.

"What did Ilsa want, Edward?" Wynne asked.

Edward was startled. He pushed his glasses back with a forefinger and shook his head. "Mrs. Hethershaw? I haven't seen her, Miss Russell."

She went into the office. For about fifteen minutes, she worked at the desk. But she was in no real mood for it. She wondered if Captain Sam might still be at the Hurricane Haven. She left the office, called good-night to Edward, and went next door. Ilsa's car was gone. Perhaps she had been at the Hurricane instead of the hotel. Wynne found Captain Sam at his usual table, having a very late supper.

"Hello, my darlin'," Sam said with his friendly grin. "Could I buy you supper?"

"I ate ages ago. Why are you so late?"

Captain Sam shrugged. "I was running behind with the ferry, and there was one thing and then another. You know how it is."

"I noticed Ilsa's car near the hotel earlier. Was she here?"

"No."

"Are you positive?"

"Listen, when Ilsa Hethershaw walks into a place or out of it everyone knows it, and she wasn't here."

Wynne frowned. Then perhaps she had been at the hotel after all. And where had Ilsa been when she walked across the lobby? But more than that, why had Edward Allen found it necessary to lie?

VII

ILSA HETHERSHAW SENT her red sports car tearing over the narrow road, roared past Priscilla Russell's place, and made for her own house, twisting the wheel as she climbed the winding road to the top of the hill. The house sprawled along the contour of the coast, hugging the earth. Palm trees gave it shade, and a few orange trees had been planted some distance from the house to the rear of the grounds. Their fragrance at blossoming time hung heavily on the air, and the surf pounded eternally at the rocks below.

Ilsa put the car in the garage and went to the house. Max was waiting for her. He stood at the sliding glass doors leading to the balcony that looked out to sea, wearing his smoking jacket, his silvery hair smoothly combed.

"Where have you been?" he asked.

"Driving. From one end of this monotonous island to the other."

"It's very late."

"So it is," she said airily.

"You know I don't like you to be out so late alone."

"What on earth could happen to me here?" she retorted. "Besides, I've told you any number of times, I'm bored."

Max was very angry. Although he stood quietly, she knew all the little signs. The clenched fists thrust into the pockets of his smoking jacket, the hot fire that leaped into his cool blue eyes and his way of standing, shoulders back, stomach pulled in.

"Where were you?"

"I stopped in at the Hurricane for a cup of coffee. Is there some law against that?"

"You know I don't like you to go there."

Ilsa spun around, her black hair swirling around her face. "You don't like for me to go anywhere! You want me to sit up here in your expensive cage like something in a zoo!"

Max stared at her. "You're seeing someone, aren't you?"

She scoffed. "Don't be ridiculous."

"I'm no fool, Ilsa. I won't tolerate it. You hear me, I won't tolerate it!"

She stepped deeper into the plush room. When Max had brought her here as his third bride, she had found the place fabulously rich. She had loved it. She had loved the idea of the remote island, living in the richest house there, being Mrs. Max Hethershaw. But it was going sour now. The glitter was wearing off. She had never had a consuming passion for Max, but she had been fond of him. She had found him interesting. But lately, he had been different. Almost frighteningly jealous. Overly possessive. A man of secrets. She knew no more about his business interests now than she had at the beginning, before they were married. He made strange phone calls. Went to Charlton on business but never told her what it was about. The few times she had protested, he had been curt, cold, almost rude.

"You're not to concern yourself with business. That's my affair."

"Are you just a little bit crooked, Max? Is that what you're hiding?"

It had been the first time he had ever struck her. She still remembered the sting of his palm against her cheek.

"How dare you say such a thing to me! I took you out of nowhere and put the best clothes on your back, money in your bank account, bought you the car of your dreams, made you somebody!"

"You can't buy everything with your money, Max. You're going to learn that someday."

Now, they were staring at each other, hostility almost a living thing between them. Ilsa turned away and opened the gold cigarette box on the coffee table and flicked the gold lighter.

"Just tell me where you were, who you saw, and what you did. Is that asking too much?"

43

She laughed hollowly. "Why don't you hire a detective to watch me, Max?"

"Don't be flip with me, Ilsa."

"I'm going to bed. Good-night."

She hurried away to her bedroom and closed the door behind her. Kicking off her shoes, she padded around in her stocking feet on the luxuriously thick carpeting, jerked at the rope to open the curtains and stepped out to her own private balcony. Egret Bay stretched beneath her, and on down the coastline, she could pick out a few of the street lights. At the very far end of the island, she knew Eric Channon's dock light was burning.

From here, she was a dizzy height above the sea, and below, the water and the jagged rocks looked menacing. In the daytime, she enjoyed sitting here, watching the sea, but at night, there was something frightening about it. She stepped back inside and found Max standing closely behind her.

"I didn't hear you!" she said.

He took another step toward her, and she stood her ground, even when she wanted to shrink away.

"Darling," he said, "I've come to apologize. I don't know what got into me. I love you so. I'm insanely jealous, and when I don't know where you are when you're so late, I imagine all sorts of things."

"You certainly do," she said coolly, but then she softened.

He smiled. He was handsome for a man his age. Of any age. It never bothered her that he was old enough to be her father. She'd always found older men more interesting. And then there was all the money, all the prestige of being Mrs. Max Hethershaw.

"Come here," he said, stretching out his arms.

With a sigh, she went to him, and he held her for a moment. She fingered the silk lapels of his smoking jacket and let him kiss her lightly.

"Forgive me?" he asked.

"Yes. Of course."

"That's my Ilsa," he laughed happily. "I've been thoughtless. I've kept you cooped up here too long. Let's do something different. We might drive to Miami."

She shook her head. "I'm bored with Miami!"

44

"Darling, I know you want to go abroad. I'd like to take you. But I simply can't this summer. There is just too much at stake."

"What's at stake? I don't understand."

"It's a business matter. I can't leave. I'm sorry. How would you like to have a party? A big lavish party? One that will set this sleepy little island on its ear?"

She stirred in his arms. "Who would we invite?"

"Anyone you want."

"Anyone?" she asked with an impish smile. "Like Captain Sam and Ruby Hammer? Edward Allen at the hotel? Priscilla Russell?"

She knew perfectly well that Max didn't truly care to associate with any of them on the island. He was a snob with a capital S. She enjoyed goading him about it.

"Do you want to invite them?"

"Why not?" she said with a laugh. "I'm sure some of them have never put a foot inside this house. Maybe it's about time."

Max reached up to rub his forefinger over his trim moustache. "Let me consider it."

She laughed. "If you want to bring some business associates over from Charlton—why not? It's fun to mix up all kinds of people."

"You have a bizarre idea of fun," Max said wryly.

"And you're a snob!" she teased. "But a pretty nice snob!"

At last, she coaxed a smile out of him. She knew she had won out. He would throw the party if she wanted it. He had forgotten all about tonight and where she had been. For another time, she had succeeded in erasing his suspicions.

"We'll discuss it again," he promised.

"Tomorrow?"

He laughed. "You really want to do this, don't you?"

"Why not? You always wanted to show me off. Why not do it properly?"

Max gave her a long look. She was never sure what was going on in that computer brain of his, or what angle he was going to put on anything.

"I am proud of you, Ilsa. You're not like anyone else I know."

She smiled to herself at that. How little he really knew about her!

"Oh, darling, before I forget. There's something wrong with my car. I had trouble starting it tonight," she told him.

"I'll have Will Dykes look at it tomorrow."

"Good! I do love my little red car."

"And me?" he asked hopefully.

"Oh, of course, Max!"

She put her arms around him and kissed him, and for tonight, at least, their quarrels were all settled.

In the morning, Ilsa slept late as usual. She heard Max leave in his car and knew that within twenty minutes or so, he would be back. He met Sam's ferry without fail and waited until Sam had sorted the mail and given it to him. The most important thing would be the *Wall Street Journal*. Max wouldn't even have a cup of coffee in the morning until he had looked at it to see how all his investments were faring.

By the time Ilsa had dressed and wandered sleepily out to the dining room, he would be there. Breakfast would be waiting, served by Mattie in stony silence. Mattie seldom made small talk. She had been with Max for many years. Ilsa knew that Mattie had never approved of her, but she didn't let it bother her. She was here, and she was Mrs. Max Hethershaw.

Max's car was coming up the drive. She heard the slam of the door, then Max's voice calling to Mattie.

"Coffee, Mattie. Please. On the patio."

Ilsa found him there, deep in the newspaper, sipping his coffee. She saw he was dressed for the city which meant he wouldn't be going sailing today. She was faced with another long, lonely day on the island.

"Good morning, darling," Max said.

"Hi."

"I stopped by Will's garage. He'll come up and see what's wrong with your car. I'm sorry, I'll have to use my car today. Sam's taking me over in an hour. But perhaps Will won't be long getting yours fixed. . . . When Lorrie comes, ask her to type the letters I left on the desk in the den."

46

"Why must you go to Charlton today?"

Max gave her a quick look. "Business. Of course. An important meeting."

"What about?" she asked with a bored voice.

"Never mind," he said. "Tell Lorrie I'll phone her some more instructions later."

"I don't see why you hired her, Max. You have your secretary in Charlton."

Max put the paper aside. "I thought you'd like to have someone young around. Someone—your age," he said. "Lorrie serves her purpose. Don't you like her?"

"Oh, she's all right, I suppose. When will you be home?"

He shot her another look. "Why do you ask?"

She sighed. "I think it is a perfectly natural thing to ask. When shall I tell Mattie to have dinner?"

"I'll phone."

"I may be out."

"Where?" he asked quickly.

"Swimming. Boating. Hiking. What else is there to do?"

"Visit the Hurricane Haven?" he asked coldly. "What's so interesting about that place?"

"Truthfully, nothing. But it's a place to go! The only place on the island that is halfway decent! We're not going to start this all over again, are we?"

Max shook his head. "No. Sorry. I'm not myself this morning. Well, I must go now. Good-bye, darling."

Ilsa lingered over the table. The long hot day stretched ahead of her. She felt restless, at loose ends. She glanced at her watch. It was time for Lorrie to come.

At last, she heard the sound of the old truck lumbering up the winding road. Lorrie came straight to the house.

"Good morning, Ilsa."

"Hi. Max left work on the desk."

"I'll get right to it. Dad's looking at your car."

"I hope he can fix it." The thought of being cooped up here all day would drive Ilsa mad in no time. When she heard Lorrie pecking away at the typewriter, Ilsa went out to the garage.

"Good morning, Will."

Will Dykes had the hood up and was poking around. He barely glanced up and made a grunting sound in greeting.

"Bad alternator," he said at last. "I'll have to order some new parts."

"You mean I can't drive it?"

"Nope. Not unless you want to get stalled somewhere."

"Oh, brother!"

Will wiped his hands on an oily rag and put the hood down. He walked back to his truck, and she followed.

"How long will it be?"

Will shrugged his bony shoulders. "Week. Ten days. Can't tell. Things are slow sometimes, and it ain't likely I can find the right part in Charlton for such a fancy little car like that."

"Well, hurry it as much as you can, will you?"

"Sure thing, Mrs. Hethershaw."

Then he turned the truck around and went rumbling away. Stuck! She was stuck here for the day. And probably a good many other days.

Fuming, she went back inside. Lorrie had stopped typing. Ilsa went to the den.

"I want you to deliver a note for me, Lorrie."

Lorrie bit her lip and lowered her head. "I'd rather not, Ilsa. Please—"

"You must!"

Lorrie was reluctant. "Ilsa, I'd rather not be involved."

"You already are!" Ilsa said angrily. "You're sworn to secrecy. If you dare tell anyone, you know what will happen."

Lorrie's face was white, and her brown eyes much too large for her face. The girl had no bargaining power, and she knew it. Ilsa had the upper hand.

"All right. I'll deliver the note when I go home tonight. Is that what you want?" Lorrie asked.

Ilsa smiled and nodded. "You're learning fast, Lorrie."

VIII

Wynne left for Tallahassee the next day and caught Captain Sam's ferry to Charlton.

"Do you think I'm a fool for coming back to stay, Sam?" she asked.

"What a terrible thing to say, my darlin'!"

"Lorrie thinks so."

Captain Sam frowned. "Lorrie's not a happy girl."

"Sam, why did she go to work on the hill?"

"Don't know. It's a job, I suppose. Max pays well. Besides, it keeps her home on the island."

"Lorrie said her father arranged it. How could Will Dykes have any influence where Max Hethershaw is concerned?"

"Now, you just asked a real dandy question, Wynne. Who knows what crawls in and out of Will's mind and how he uses it. I don't trust him any further than you can throw an elephant."

It was raining when Wynne reached Charlton, and she had a bumpy plane ride back to Tallahassee. The rain followed all the way. She went straight to the office and as quickly as she could, went to see Jack Brown. He flashed her a welcoming smile.

"Wynne! You're back. Emergency all taken care of?"

"Jack, I hate to say this, but I'm going back to Feather Island to operate the South Wind Hotel. My grandmother owns it. She needs me."

Jack took this all in with a stony face. "No chance you'd reconsider?"

"No. I'm sorry. I'd like to leave as quickly as possible. Today. Tomorrow."

"All right. But I hate to see you go."

"If you ever come to Feather Island, I'll see to it that you have the best room in the hotel."

Jack rolled a pencil under his palm across the top of his desk. A little smile played around his mouth.

"You know, Wynne, you might be seeing me before you expect it." He got to his feet and stretched out his hand. His fingers closed around hers warmly. "I'll miss you, Wynne. But good luck. With everything."

She hurried away and went back to her own office. She spent an hour there, putting things in order, gathering her belongings and saying good-bye to everyone.

The apartment took longer. She decided to spend the night there and get an early start in the morning. The drive back on the interstate seemed a long one alone, and she wished more and more that Lorrie had been able to come with her.

She reached Charlton in time to catch the five o'clock ferry that evening. She had skipped lunch, anxious to get the miles out of the way. Now, she realized how hungry she was. There was a small diner nearby, and she went there. A cup of coffee would tide her over until dinner time.

The diner was a meeting place for people waiting for the ferry. She saw a few island acquaintances and talked with them. Then before she had finished her coffee, a stranger came in. A tall, rangy man with brown hair and an outdoor look about him. Dark glasses hid his eyes. For the barest moment, she was certain she knew him. Then when she could put no name to him, she decided she had been mistaken.

Sam arrived, and Wynne saw the stranger drive his car aboard the ferry.

"Hello, Wynne!" Sam shouted. "Happy to see you're back."

"Did you miss me?"

"You'd better believe it," Sam laughed. "Say, I want to talk to you after we get under way."

Wynne left her car and went to stand at the rail. The evening breeze was refreshing. Perhaps yesterday's rain had cooled things off for a few days. The stranger stood just a few feet away. Now and then, he gave her a curious

50

glance, and she gave him a casual smile. Why did he seem so familiar? He wore tan work clothes. Heavy shoes. A straw hat. His hands on the railing were suntanned, lean, but had a look of strength about them. He was no ordinary tourist, she was sure of that. Perhaps he had come to visit somebody on Feather Island. Perhaps he had been here before.

When the ferry was well under way, she went to talk with Sam as he handled the wheel.

"I want to know what's up," Sam said. "Why the meeting at your grandmother's house tonight?"

"What meeting?" Wynne asked with surprise.

Sam shrugged and pushed his cap to the back of his head. "That's what I'm asking you. I only know Wilma called and told me to be there. Not just me either. Several of the others have been asked too. Nine o'clock."

Wynne took a deep breath. Grandmother was up to something. Wynne wished she had waited. Discussed it with her. But it was something Grandmother would do. She was still the force behind things. Dad had resented it at times. Welcomed it at others. Wynne, frankly, didn't know how she would feel about it.

"Excuse me." The tall stranger stood there. "I'm going to the South Wind Hotel," he said. "Could you give me directions?"

Wynne was startled. She knew of no reservation for anyone new, but then, it could have come in yesterday while she was away.

"You're looking at the manager," Captain Sam said with a nod toward Wynne. "This is Miss Russell."

"I'm Scott Stoner. Would you be able to accommodate me, Miss Russell?"

"Yes, and if you'll follow me when we leave the ferry, I'll take you there."

Scott Stoner gave her a smile. His teeth were very white in his suntanned face. She wished she could see his eyes behind the dark glasses.

He gave her a nod and moved away.

"Do you know him, Sam?" Wynne asked.

"Never heard of him. Seems to me the island is getting full of strangers."

Wynne laughed. "The only other stranger there is Brad Sherman."

Captain Sam scowled and with one hand gripped the wheel and with the other lighted his stub pipe.

"Speaking of Brad. Just what is he looking for out there in the ocean?"

"He likes to dive. A hobby."

"I wonder if that's all there is to it," Captain Sam said. "I hear he's got some pretty fancy equipment. He can go deep. Real deep. What's he expecting to find? One of those old U-boats that sunk out there years ago?"

"I suspect he is just a romantic at heart. He seems infatuated with the sea and what it holds. He calls it another world down there. In fact, he wants me to go diving with him."

Captain Sam stared at her. "You know better, don't you? That's dangerous business! You're inexperienced! Now, I taught you a good many things about the sea, but I never taught you any diving—"

She laughed and put a hand on his arm. "Easy, Sam. I said no."

"Just seems strange. Never had anybody so busy looking at our ocean before."

When they reached Feather Island, Wynne waited until Scott Stoner had pulled up behind her, and then she drove to the hotel. Edward was behind the desk when she went in.

"We have a new guest. Would you help him with his luggage?"

Edward was always so efficient. Sometimes, he unnerved her with his perfectionist ways. She sometimes wished he would make a mistake so she would know he was human like everyone else.

Scott's luggage consisted of several odd suitcases. Not the usual luggage. They looked as if they might contain instruments or perhaps samples.

At the desk, she gave Scott one of the better rooms, and he signed the register with a quick, firm hand. He gave his address as St. Augustine, Florida.

Edward took the luggage and led the new guest up to his room. The phone was ringing. It was Grandmother.

"Wynne, I'm glad you got back," she said. "I'll want you at the house at nine o'clock. It's important."

"I heard about the meeting from Sam. Grandmother, what's it all about?"

"I'll tell you in good time."

Then the line went dead, and with a touch of red-headed anger, Wynne slammed the receiver. Why was she being kept in the dark? A few minutes later, she phoned Lorrie and asked her to come to the Hurricane for dinner.

"I really shouldn't, Wynne. I have to fix a meal here—"

"Fix it and then come," Wynne said. "Please. I want to talk with you."

Lorrie seemed hesitant. Then finally, she agreed.

Wynne had the chore of carrying in all her belongings from the car to the apartment at the rear of the South Wind. There had been some happy times spent here in the past. Sad ones as well. It would be very strange without Dad.

When she had carried everything in from the car, she was too tired to unpack very much. She took a quick shower, put on a fresh dress, and went across to the Hurricane. It was five minutes of seven. Lorrie had not arrived.

Maude Pearson was playing the piano in her usual bouncy style. She taught music in Charlton and played only a few nights a week for Ruby. But when she was there, she gave the place a lift, her merry blue eyes twinkling, and her fingers dancing over the keyboard. Maude was no spring chicken and once had designs on Captain Sam, but to no avail.

"Hello, Wynne!" Maude called. She went right on playing, never missing a note.

Ruby came with a menu, but Wynne told her she was waiting for Lorrie. She had a choice table where she could watch the last of the sunset on the water. By seven-thirty, Lorrie still had not come, but Brad Sherman arrived. He came bearing down on her. "I was hoping you'd get back today."

"Some special reason? Something wrong at the hotel? Did Johnny Dykes come to see you?"

53

"Johnny came. I hired him. He seems like a good kid. We've been out already, and he learns fast. The hotel is fine. My room is fine. Just one thing wrong."

"Oh?"

He smiled at her, and she saw the silvery specks in his blue eyes.

"It's intolerably lonely," he said.

"I'm sorry, the hotel doesn't have a social director."

"Sure it does. You," Brad said with a warm smile. "How would you like to go over to Charlton in the *Lazy Day* after dinner?"

"Can't. Sorry."

"Another time?"

"Perhaps. Did you make a dive today?"

"A couple. I truly believe the water at Dolphin Bay is the clearest I've ever seen."

Dolphin Bay! She felt her smile fade away. A thud echoed against her heart. She could never think of Dolphin Bay without remembering Eric Channon.

"Did I say something wrong?"

"Of course not. I'm glad you like the island. Have you found any hidden pirate's treasure?"

He laughed. "No. But when I do, I'll give you all the jewels. I promise."

"There *were* pirates once. Long ago. At least, that's what I've always heard," Wynne said.

Brad looked interested. "And once the Spanish owned the island."

"That's right. So, you've been reading up on Feather Island!"

"Sure. During all those cold winter nights in North Dakota, it was fun to read about places like Feather Island."

Wynne glanced at her watch. Lorrie wasn't coming. She wouldn't be this late.

"Were you waiting for someone?" Brad asked.

"Yes. But I've given her up now. Johnny's sister. Lorrie."

"Then shall we order?"

Ruby served them a delicious dinner, and Brad told her about North Dakota. "You should see the evening shadows on the snow," he said. "And the sky when it's all rosy and the snow changes colors right before your eyes. And the icicles. Two- or three-feet long hanging from the schoolhouse roof! Then there are the sleigh rides when you bundle up in a fur robe and the popcorn and hot chocolate afterwards. Not to mention the cold, long nights in front of a fireplace, reading—"

"I know what you are. You're a dreamer! You've got stardust in your eyes, Brad Sherman."

"Maybe I'm not a realist as much as I should be. But I enjoy life."

Maude missed a note, and surprised, Wynne looked up. She saw the reason at once. Isla Hethershaw had come into the room. Everyone noticed her. Ilsa looked neither left nor right, but took the first empty booth. Ruby waited on her personally and in a moment, carried her a cup of coffee. Ilsa looked very lonely, sitting there by herself, paying no attention to anyone. At last, she got up, took her cup with her, and went to lean against Maude's piano.

"Play something blue, Maude. That's the way I feel tonight."

Maude nodded and swung into some of the old standards that had come out of New Orleans, low, sweet, and moody. Ilsa sipped her coffee and listened, a faraway look in her eyes.

"Who is she?" Brad asked. "I think I saw her around the hotel the other day."

"Ilsa Hethershaw. She lives in the big house on the hill."

"Max Hethershaw's daughter?" Brad asked with interest.

"Wife."

Brad lifted his brows with surprise. "Now, talk about misplaced souls, Wynne, there's one if I ever saw it!"

Ilsa was still there when they'd finished eating. By then, the time had whiled away to eight-thirty. Wynne knew she must leave now if she wanted to be at Grandmother's house on time.

Just as she was ready to go, she spied Lorrie, who paused in the doorway, a small girl who always looked as if she had been halted in mid flight.

"Wynne!" she said, coming to the table quickly. "I'm sorry I'm so late. I just couldn't get away."

Brad got to his feet. He towered over Lorrie by a good foot. How tiny Lorrie seemed standing beside him.

"And I'm just leaving," Wynne said. "Lorrie, this is Brad Sherman."

"So, you're Johnny's big sister," Brad said, extending his big hand. "Johnny didn't tell me you were so tiny. Sit down. Have some coffee with me."

Wynne left them knowing that Brad had probably already engaged Lorrie in a discussion about diving. His company would be good for Lorrie.

Wynne got into her car and drove away toward her grandmother's house, apprehensive and curious.

IX

A LIGHT BURNED brightly at the house, and Wynne saw that several other cars were already parked there. She hurried up to the door and lifted the knocker. Then without waiting for Wilma to answer, she stepped inside. She heard voices. They had all gathered in the living room, and Grandmother sat there, cane in her hand, her white head held regally.

"Come in, Wynne. Sit down," Grandmother said.

Benson, who operated the grocery, sat stiffly in one of the formal chairs. Walker, who ran the laundry, and the Ward brothers, who operated a pharmacy, sat huddled together on the divan, looking dubious and uneasy. Michaels, who rented boats, stirred in his chair, moving his feet constantly. Only Captain Sam, bless him, seemed perfectly at ease. He sat relaxed, feet out, his seaman's cap resting on the arm of the easy chair, his stub pipe in his mouth. A couple of other people were long time residents of the island and owned large chunks of land.

Ruby Hammer was the last to arrive, coming in just a few minutes behind Wynne. Then Grandmother rapped the floor with her cane.

"I've called you all here for a purpose. A good purpose. I've been to a lawyer at Charlton. He'll try to help. I know all of you here feel as I do. The first thing that must be done is for all of you to sign a petition. The papers have been drawn up."

It took Wynne only a moment to understand what the meeting was about. Of course, the bridge!

"What good will signing a paper do, ma'am?" Michaels asked.

"It will be sent to the proper people. I'll see to it. I have friends in Tallahassee, and I know the man in charge

57

of the highway commission. Personally I think our protests will be listened to and considered."

"They're going to come with it," Benson spoke up. "No matter what we say. Begging your pardon, Mrs. Russell, I don't reckon even you can stop it."

There was a babble of voices. Everyone tried to talk at once. Grandmother rapped the floor sharply with her cane, and silence reigned.

"We all have reasons not to want the bridge. We all know what kind of changes it would bring. I've taken the initiative on this. I expect all of you to follow."

They exchanged glances around the room. Then Captain Sam got to his feet.

"None of us are getting rich, but we aren't in the poor house either. We all like Feather Island just as it is. That right, everybody?"

The talk started again. In a moment, Grandmother was motioning to Wynne. She thrust the paper into her hand.

"Read this aloud, then pass it around, and have them all sign it."

It was a simple petition. Wynne read it, and everyone listened closely. Then it was passed from one to the other, and everyone put their signature to it.

"By golly," Sam said, rubbing his hands. "We're not just going to stand here and let them ruin the island. We're going to fight. Three cheers for Mrs. Russell!"

Grandmother endured Sam's praise without blinking an eye. Then nervously, Benson got to his feet and said goodnight. Everyone else followed as if eager to be gone.

Ruby paused beside Wynne. She fingered the bun of brown hair at the nape of her neck. "Do you think we've got a chance, Wynne? Just between you and me?"

"I hope so, Ruby."

"I'd hate to have to give up or sell out."

Wynne gave Ruby a tired smile, a kind of sick dread in her heart. Give up or sell out? Those two things struck terror to the depths of her soul. No. She would never give up. She would never sell out! Then she laughed to herself. That was what Grandmother would say! Was she so much like the old lady after all? Eric had accused her of it.

At last, all had gone. Grandmother got stiffly to her feet. She grasped the petition tightly in her hand.

"I'll take care of this tomorrow."

"Grandmother—do you really think you have any influence in Tallahassee?"

"Of course! I most certainly have."

"I wish you had told me you were doing this."

Grandmother ignored the statement. "Will you stay for tea?"

"No. I can't. Good night, Grandmother."

She left the house, her thoughts in a whirl. She went back to the Hurricane, but Lorrie had gone. She decided to drive to her house. Somehow she couldn't get Lorrie out of her mind.

She took the familiar road to the bay side of the island. A light burned in Lorrie's house, and when she reached it, she hurried to knock at the door. It was late. But it didn't matter. She was determined to speak with Lorrie.

Will opened the door.

"Is Lorrie here?"

"Busy in the kitchen," he said. "What was all the cars doing at your grandma's place?"

She started to tell him and then suddenly realized Will was the only businessman on the island that hadn't attended the meeting. Why? Because Grandmother hadn't asked him!

She ignored Will's question, brushed past him, and went to the kitchen. Lorrie was finishing the dishes and gave her a quick, guarded look. But it wasn't quick enough. Wynne's heart turned over. Lorrie had been crying.

"Lorrie, what is it?"

"Nothing."

"It wasn't Brad Sherman?"

"Of course not! He was very nice. He wanted to take me for a ride in the *Lazy Day*."

"It might have been fun," Wynne pointed out. "I think you could use some fun."

Lorrie went right on drying the dishes, making a little more noise than necessary.

"Are you going to tell me what's wrong?"

"Will you stop pestering me?" Lorrie snapped.

Wynne bit her lip. Lorrie seldom got angry. And never at her.

"I'm sorry. I only wanted to help. All right. I'll go. It's been a very long day. Listen, how about lunch Sunday? A picnic lunch. Like we used to have."

Lorrie swallowed hard and nodded. Wynne knew that Lorrie was sorry for her abruptness. "OK," she said.

Wynne said good-night and left quickly before Will could detain her with more questions. She felt uneasy, uncertain. And somehow frightened.

Scott Stoner had settled in his hotel room, unpacking his things in an efficient, methodical way. He wished he had a dollar for every time he had done this. After seven years of moving around, of sleeping in hotel rooms and eating restaurant food, he was sick of it. But it went with his job, and the job compensated for other losses.

He got in his car and drove around the island, up and down each road on his map. It was just a small piece of earth in the huge ocean with plenty of trees, birds, and sand. It was truly a lovely spot. They'd been right about that.

About nine o'clock, he drove back to the hotel, parked his car and went next door for a late supper. As he was leaving, he met a tiny young lady with brown eyes and a quick smile. She was followed by Brad Sherman. Scott had met him earlier at the hotel.

The supper was a good one. It surprised him a little. Most restaurant food left him still hungry and dissatisfied. When he'd finished, he decided to go down to the beach in front of the hotel.

The stars were out, and there was a small slice of moon. The surf rippled silver at his feet. He walked slowly, enjoying the night air. Then suddenly, just ahead of him he saw a small hump on the sand. It moved, and in a moment, a wild barking started up.

"Quiet down, pooch," Scott laughed. "What's the matter? I won't hurt you."

The dog came cautiously toward him. Scott stroked the furry head, fingered the lop ears, and felt for a collar. But there was none.

"Why don't you go on home now?"

But the dog was determined to stay. As Scott walked on, the dog followed. Several times, Scott scolded him and tried to send him away. But the dog persisted.

When Scott returned to the hotel, it was past ten o'clock. A night-light burned in the lobby, and no one was at the desk. The dog was determined to go inside with him.

"Pet's aren't allowed, pooch," Scott laughed.

He closed the door and looked back. The dog looked pathetic, head down, tail sagging. He whimpered in an agonizing way, and Scott shook his head.

"Of all things!" he murmured.

He went back to his car, opened the door, and motioned for the dog to jump in.

"You can sleep there. OK?"

The dog licked his hand in gratitude. With a laugh, Scott went back to the lobby. Wynne Russell was coming out of the office.

"Good evening," he said. "I wonder if you could help me."

"Of course. What is it?"

"I went walking on the beach and came back with a dog. He won't go home. I wonder if you might know his owner. I've got him out in the car."

She followed him outside, and the dog barked in delight when Wynne petted him for a moment.

"What a cute little dog! But I'm sorry, I don't know him. Perhaps he's a stray. Sometimes people bring dogs over here and leave them, hoping someone will give them a home. It's happened before."

Scott nodded. "Perhaps. Well, I'll keep him a couple of days to see if anyone claims him."

"Do you often take up with stray dogs?" Wynne asked lightly.

"I'm a sucker for a cute face, and this one has one," Scott laughed. "I never had a pet as a kid. I always wanted a dog. Or a horse or even a cat. I never had any of them."

Scott looked at Wynne Russell, a tall, redheaded young woman with smoky gray eyes and a pretty smile. Piano music was spilling out to the darkness from next door. It struck a plaintive note inside Scott's heart. He felt undeniably lonely standing here beside Wynne Russell, wishing he knew her better, wishing he could ask her to go for a walk or to have a cup of coffee—anything to keep her close by.

But she gave him a quick smile and said good-night. "I hope you find his owner."

"Miss Russell—"

"Yes?"

"Would you have dinner with me tomorrow night?"

She was startled. "I'm sorry. I'll be on duty tomorrow night. My assistant, Mr. Allen, has been serving double time for several days now."

"Another time?" he asked, not about to be put off. "I'll ask another time."

X

WILL DYKES KNEW there was something in the wind. When Wynne left, he went out to the kitchen. Lorrie was just finishing up with the dishes.

"What did she want?" he asked.

Lorrie gave him a quick look. "Nothing much. We're going on a picnic Sunday."

"Did she call the meeting tonight, or did her grandma?"

"I wouldn't know."

"What was it all about?"

Lorrie slammed down the dish towel with disgust. "How should I know?"

"You find out."

Lorrie laughed bitterly. "How do you expect me to do that?"

"You work up at the big house on the hill. Ain't nothing goes on this island that Max Hethershaw doesn't know about."

"The way you talk, Max Hethershaw owns the whole island! Well, he doesn't!"

Will scratched at his day-old beard. "He don't even own his own wife, the way I hear it."

"What do you mean?"

"Ilsa Hethershaw's asking for trouble, ain't she?"

Lorrie looked pale and uncertain.

"I don't know what you're talking about."

Will laughed and sauntered away. Sometimes, he wondered how he could have a daughter that was so dumb. How did Lorrie think he got her a job up there? Just by asking? Not hardly. Hethershaw didn't do anyone on the island any favors without a reason. And Will reckoned he'd given Hethershaw plenty of reasons.

By chance, Will had happened by the Russell place

earlier and seen all the cars. He'd recognized most of them. There wasn't an automobile, bicycle, truck, or vehicle of any kind on the island that he didn't know. At one time or another he had worked on most of them. It looked like there had been some kind of town meeting going on. Everybody had been there but him! Well, he'd see about that!

He walked over to Sam's place and found the office locked and the light out. Sam kept a small apartment around to the rear. He went there and pounded at the door.

"Hey, Sam. Roust it out!" he yelled.

In a moment, Sam opened the door, scowling at him.

"What is it, Will?"

Will pushed the door open with a rough shove, and Sam stepped back. Sam had his shirt unbuttoned and looked as if he were getting ready for bed.

"I'd like a word with you, Sam."

"Now?" Sam said. "I'm about ready for bed. It's late."

"Not that late," Will said.

Sam had a nice place here. He kept it as clean as a ship in the navy. Sam never forgot that he'd gone to sea during World War II and had come back something of a hero. Pictures of his ship hung on the wall, and there were mementoes hanging everywhere.

"I see you went to a little meeting tonight, Sam," Will said.

Sam was on guard. He went to find his stub pipe and fill it.

"Mrs. Russell sort of forgot to invite somebody, didn't she?" Will asked.

"No," Sam said, giving him a level look.

Will bristled. He felt the heat begin at the base of his throat and climb to his face. Nobody wanted Will Dykes around unless their car wouldn't start or some engine needed repairs. It had always been this way. Dirt. He was dirt to the high and mighties!

"Now, Will, it's late, and I'm in no mood to argue with you about anything," Sam said.

But Will wasn't budging. He took a wicker chair and stretched out his legs. His boots were bursting at the seams, and the heels were run over. Someday, he reckoned he'd have to see about getting a new pair. It was just one of those things he'd get around to eventually.

"Now, Sam, we're neighbors," Will said, digging out a toothpick from his shirt pocket and inspecting his teeth with it one at a time. "I reckon you owe me a favor or two."

"I owe you nothing, Will. I pay my bills."

Will laughed shortly. "That you do, Sam. Better than some. I reckon I ain't the most social man on the island, but if I was having a little tea party, wouldn't you have liked to have had an invite?"

"It was no tea party," Sam said.

Will finished with the toothpick and snapped it between his fingers. Sam was playing it close. But there were ways of finding out things. Will got to his feet and moved to the door.

"I'll remember this, Sam."

Sam's blue eyes shot fire for a moment. Then with another laugh, Will left. He stood for a moment, looking over at Charlton. Wouldn't be long now. The bridge would be coming. Horse sense told him it would reach Feather Island in a spot that would bring the new road right by his garage. He'd open up a new gas station and have the best business spot on the island! He grinned thinking about it. On top of that, they'd have to buy some right-of-way from him. If a man knew what he was doing, he could hold out and get the price he wanted. Maybe, just maybe, the chips were going to start falling for Will Dykes for a change.

He went back to the house and climbed into the old truck. It rattled and sputtered all the way down the road toward Hurricane Haven. It needed some work, but he didn't take time to do it. It had been ready for the junkyard the last year or so, and by sheer know-how, he'd kept it running. It didn't do to let folks on the island think he had money for a new truck. They never would pay their bills. Besides, he knew there was no one else on the island like him. It made him unique. Important. He enjoyed it. Whether they wanted to admit it or not, Will Dykes was someone special. Even Hethershaw was finding that out.

He saw the lights of the South Wind Hotel and the

neon sign of the Hurricane. He parked the truck and went into the Hurricane. Maude was there, thumping the piano. Will stopped to pat her on the shoulder and grin at her.

"Well, look who's here," Maude said.

"I want to see Ruby. She's back from the meeting, ain't she?"

Maude's eyes were veiled. "She's in the kitchen."

Will went to sit down at one of the tables. One of Ruby's waitresses, a pretty little thing who lived near Dolphin Bay, came sashaying by, and he reached out to jerk at her apron strings.

"Hi, honey. Bring me a cup of coffee, will you? And a piece of pie."

"This isn't my table."

She was annoyed, and Will laughed. In a few minutes, Ruby appeared. She plunked the coffee and the pie down in front of him.

"Stop bothering the girls, Will. I've told you before."

"Here, here. Let's not be nasty, Ruby. I'm a customer. Sit down and join me."

"I've things to do in the kitchen."

Will pulled out a chair. "Sit down, Ruby. You'd better hear both sides of it."

"I don't know what you mean. Now, if you'll excuse me—"

"You were to Russell's tonight, weren't you? You and just about everybody else that ain't in favor of the bridge."

Ruby sat down. "What's it to you?"

"What was the meeting all about? How come they didn't invite me?"

"It wasn't my meeting," Ruby said. "I don't want to talk about it, Will."

"Reckon you'd better," Will said. "You'd better think twice. The big man on the hill—he wants the bridge. Did you know that?"

"No. And neither do you, Will. You're all bluff."

Will held up two fingers, crossed. "We're like that, Ruby. Ain't you noticed. Got my girl workin' up there, ain't I? How do you think I managed that unless me and Max are buddies?"

Ruby stared at him. Will laughed and tasted the pie.

"Real good, Ruby. You still bake them yourself?"

"Will, what do you want?"

"Just a little friendly warning because I reckon you're one of the prettiest women on the island, Ruby."

She made a face at that. It was true, though. She was one nice hunk of woman. Will liked a woman with some meat on her bones. He suspected from way back that Ruby had some Spanish blood.

"Get on with it, Will."

Will drank deeply from his cup of coffee.

"It's like this. I'd be careful what I did and what I said. Max will get wind of it, you know that. He always does. And he won't take kindly to it."

"I couldn't care less about Max," Ruby pointed out. "He can live up there in his smug little house with his fancy wife for all I care."

Will dabbed at his lips daintily with a napkin and wadded it between his hands. He dropped it in the middle of his plate and pushed back from the table.

"You line up against him, and you'll be sorry. In more ways than one."

Then Will walked over to the cash register, helped himself to a handful of mints and a fresh toothpick, and grinned at Ruby over his shoulder.

"Put it on my tab, Ruby."

Then he stepped out into the warm night breeze and went back to his truck. Ruby would spread the word. If she didn't, he'd do it himself. Max would be pleased when he heard about it. Max would be grateful. And right now, he wanted to stay on the good side of Max Hethershaw.

Maybe he'd take a run up that way. Just to look around. It paid to keep his eyes open. Wasn't that the way he'd spotted Ilsa that night? Hadn't he turned that little tidbit into something pretty good?

The truck made a lot of noise as it rambled up the road toward the Hethershaw house. A short distance away from the drive leading to the house, he pulled off into the trees and killed the motor. He went the rest of the way on foot, taking a shortcut through the palms, coming out to a cleared area near the house. They called it Sunset Point. From here, standing high on the cliff, he had a dizzy look at the water below. A treacherous place. It gave him the whim-whams. He moved back, watching his step.

As he approached the house, he stayed in the shadows. Everything was quiet. A quick look in the garage and he saw both cars were there. Ilsa was staying home to-night.

He'd about decided to go when he heard the boat. It was coming around the far end of the island, but homing in on Hethershaw's landing dock. It was moving slowly, making as little noise as possible.

"Reckon I'll stick around awhile," Will said to himself. "See who it is."

He hunched under a tree, watching. A brighter light came on, brilliant in the darkness, and Will saw the man climb out of the boat, carrying a briefcase. Then Max came to meet him, to shake his hand. They moved away into the darkness toward the steps leading up to the house. Will scratched at his whiskers. Couldn't get a good enough look. But the man seemed familiar somehow. Somebody from Charlton more than likely. But why come at this time of night like a thief, slipping into Egret Bay? Only one reason. Hethershaw was up to something. Something he didn't want the rest of the island to know about. Something he didn't want to handle in Charlton.

Will hitched himself up to his full, stringy height and decided not to risk going closer to the house. It was enough for now that he knew about this strange visit. He could use it. Drop it out in the line of conversation, a hint, a half-truth, just as he had about Ilsa. And look what that had gained him!

XI

THE NEXT MORNING, Wynne began to tackle the paper work that had piled up on her father's desk. She had a conference with the McCalls. Pete had an estimate for the paint. It made her eyes hurt just to look at it. What a dent that would make in their cash reserve, which she had already learned was much lower than she had expected.

"And you, Marge?"

"I've got a list as long as your arm, Wynne. Are you ready for it?"

Marge had found something to be done in nearly every room. Everything from putting down new carpeting, to new curtains, to new plumbing. Not to mention four mattresses that needed replacing, a linen supply that was short and two broken air conditioning units.

"Is it that bad, Marge?"

"I'll take you on a tour of the rooms if you want."

"No. I believe you. Regretfully," she sighed. "I'll see what can be done. Perhaps we'll be able to fix some of the rooms at least."

"Your father tried several times. Your grandmother wouldn't listen."

"I'll give it a try, just the same."

Would Grandmother agree to make even a few changes? Wynne had her doubts. Small, necessary things, yes. Large things, no. It was as if tearing out old plumbing and old carpeting would somehow change the character of the South Wind. Grandmother wanted it as it was. A quaint, rather picturesque place on the sea where old friends would find it as they remembered it.

There was a knock at the office door, and she looked up to see Ruby Hammer.

It was very unusual for Ruby to come here. She almost never left her restaurant except to go home. Now, Ruby lowered her large frame into a chair in front of the desk. She seemed nervous and upset.

"Wynne, I want you to do me a favor. Blot out my name on the petition. I want it off."

Wynne was stunned. "But why? What's happened. Last night—"

"Last night I was a fool!" Ruby burst out angrily. "I just want my name taken off. Is that too much to ask?"

"You should tell Grandmother, not me."

Ruby jabbed a hairpin deeper into the bun at the nape of her neck and took a deep breath.

"When I came here from Miami, I thought I'd found paradise. I like the island as it is. Everyone knows that. But I'm just one little person. We're all *little* people. How can we hold out against the big people?"

"Grandmother has influence. I'm sure the petition will do some good."

"We're all just whistling in the dark!" Ruby said.

"What's changed your mind so quickly? Why have you reversed your position? Are you saying you want the bridge?"

"No. No!" Ruby said angrily. "Of course not. But it's like this. I'll be years paying off the Hurricane. I went deeply in debt to buy the place. I got my loan from the Charlton Trust. You know who owns that bank, don't you?"

Wynne felt a chill go over her. "Max Hethershaw!"

"I didn't sleep a wink last night. How can we fight Max Hethershaw? Everyone says he wants the bridge. You don't know how hot people are about this. It's almost come to blows between some of them. People who have been friends for years are no longer speaking."

Wynne nodded.

"Please ask your grandmother to remove my name from the petition."

Wynne said she would, and decided the sooner she discussed a few things with Grandmother the better. As she was leaving the hotel, she saw Scott coming out of the Hurricane next door. Then he opened the door to his car, and the little stray dog came leaping out into his arms.

70

"Hey, are you that hungry?" Scott asked.

Wynne went over to take a better look at the dog in the broad light of day. He was adorable. His coat was thick and soft, his eyes round and bright. A little black nose poked up through the shaggy white fur with a high shine.

"I think I've got a new friend," Scott laughed. "Will it be all right if I keep him?"

"There's a hotel rule. No pets inside."

"I'll let him sleep here in the car."

"I've no objections to that. Are you convinced he's a stray?"

"No collar. No tag. I've asked around, no one knows anything about him," Scott said.

There was almost an air of relief in his voice. Wynne watched the dog eat the scraps Scott had begged from Ruby and knew she must not dally any longer. The morning was slipping away.

The short drive to her grandmother's house wasn't long enough for her to get herself prepared for the meeting. Wilma opened the door at her knock.

"She's on the veranda," Wilma said.

"What kind of mood—"

Wilma laughed. "She's very pleased with herself right now. The petition, you know."

Wynne went through the house to the veranda. Grandmother was having a cup of tea.

"Will you join me?"

"No, thank you. I had a big breakfast at the Hurricane. I must restock my cupboards and cook in the apartment. Dad left the place bare—"

She broke off. Grandmother's face had gone dark and foreboding at the mention of her father.

"What is it you want, Wynne?"

"First, about the petition—"

"It's gone. In the morning mail. I sent Wilma down to the post office with it, and Captain Sam has carried it over to Charlton. I should have a reply in a few days."

Ruby was too late! At least Wynne was spared the trouble of telling Grandmother that she had changed her mind.

"You really think—"

Grandmother rapped the floor harshly. "Of course! I know a man at the highway commission personally. He owes me a favor."

"But what if it doesn't work, Grandmother?"

Grandmother clinked her cup to her saucer. "Then I shall find another way!"

Wynne didn't want to argue. For the first time that she could remember, Grandmother was putting on blinders. She was only seeing half the picture. Progress was hard to stop, and most people, despite the few on Feather Island who liked their privacy, were in favor of moving forward.

"I've been checking things at the hotel. We need repairs, some freshening up. I have a list."

"Leave it. I'll look at it later."

"All right. I hope you'll go along with this, Grandmother. The hotel is getting shabby."

"Nonsense! You young people all think alike. Everything has to be all bright and shiny and new. Old things have their own charm, their own worth."

It seemed pointless to argue. Wynne got to her feet and said good-bye.

"I'll expect you Sunday noon for lunch."

Wynne shook her head. "I've already made plans."

She saw the displeasure cross her grandmother's face.

"Lorrie and I are going on a picnic, like we used to do, remember?"

Grandmother pursed her lips. "Whatever is that girl doing up at the Hethershaw house?"

"Working. As a social secretary."

"Social secretary!" Grandmother scoffed. "Ilsa is in no more need of a social secretary than I am."

"Then why is she there?"

Grandmother grasped her cane tightly. "I'm sure I wouldn't know what Max has in mind or why. Or why Will Dykes was running around up here so late last night in that noisy old truck of his."

"Will was up this way last night?"

"Yes. After the meeting. I'll never know how Will Dykes could have a daughter like Lorrie."

On that note, Wynne said good-bye and left.

Sunday was typically bright and warm. Wynne had spoken with Lorrie on the phone and promised to pick her up about eleven, complete with swimsuit, suntan oil, and sunglasses.

When Wynne left the hotel, Edward manning the desk, she realized how much she had missed doing things like this. It made her feel very young and optimistic. Lorrie would always be a part of the golden memories. The good days. The good times.

Lorrie was ready and waiting. As they drove away, Lorrie told her how grateful she was for Johnny's job.

"He's so excited and happy about it. Brad pays him well. It keeps him occupied. Dad wants to make a mechanic out of him. Johnny couldn't be less interested."

"Don't they get along any better?"

"No," Lorrie shook her head. "It's a worry."

"Brad will be a good influence on Johnny. Being a teacher, he knows how to handle young people."

Lorrie smiled. "Yes. I know. He talked about his teaching. But mostly, he talked about diving. The man's obsessed!"

"Where shall we go?" Wynne asked. "You decide."

"The old lighthouse," Lorrie said quickly. "I haven't been there in ages."

Wynne's throat tightened. The lighthouse was on the southernmost point of the island and to reach it, they had to go directly past Eric's house and the clear, green waters of Dolphin Bay. From the lighthouse, Eric's place was visible, and with it were all the things she no longer cared to remember.

They drove along slowly, not caring when they got there. It was one of the qualities of the island. People knew how to relax here. Wynne, in the short few years she'd been away, had nearly forgotten.

"Oh, look!" Lorrie said.

A huge pelican had come soaring across the highway, bound for the water just a few feet from the road. He was such an awkward, ugly bird that they laughed. They saw him hit the water with a splash.

As they neared Eric's house, Wynne found herself gripping the wheel tightly. It hurt just looking at it. It was a modern structure, oddly shaped by the standard of most houses on the island, but it had a marvelous view of the bay and was very efficient and comfortable.

Eric's car was in the drive, and his boat was in the dock. He was home. For one crazy moment, Wynne wanted to turn in as she had once, go rushing up to the door to shout hello to him. She wanted to hear his steps coming quickly to let her in, she wanted to feel his arms pulling her close, his lips claiming hers.

Her eyes were stinging with tears. Lorrie's hand covered hers on the wheel.

"I'm sorry. How thoughtless can I be? We should have gone somewhere else for the picnic."

Wynne shook her head. "No. There had to be a first time, I suppose."

"Are you still so crazy about him?"

"One day, I hate him. The next day—well, I don't hate him quite so much. Another time, I ache with loneliness for him. Does that answer your question?"

"You always did lead with your heart, Wynne. In this world, you have to have a hard head too."

"Do you?" Wynne asked.

"I try."

It was on the tip of Wynne's tongue to ask questions, to pry out the reason for her tears that night in the kitchen. But Wynne was determined not to pry. When Lorrie was ready, she would tell her about it.

The lighthouse came into view. It stood there in a kind of quiet majesty. It was no longer in use. A high wire fence protected it from the curious. The islanders were fond of it. Proud of it. They wanted to preserve it, for it belonged here. Beyond, the white sand beach shimmered in the sun. But the breeze was cool as they stretched out beach towels and blankets. They decided on a quick dip before lunch. They peeled down to swimsuits, laughing and shouting to each other. The surf rolled in, foaming across the sand, and the gulls screeched overhead, sensing there was food and hoping for a handout later.

They raced each other into the water, and they splashed in, letting the water take them, swimming hard and fast, meeting the waves as they came rolling in.

For half an hour, they challenged each other to races and finally, tired, let the surf carry them back to their picnic lunch.

"Oh, that was fun. Do you know I've hardly been swimming this summer," Lorrie said.

"That's not right," Wynne scolded gently. "You ought to have a little fun once in awhile."

"Well—"

Wynne held her breath. It was going to come now. Any moment, Lorrie was going to break down and tell her. But then abruptly, Lorrie's mood changed.

"We'd better eat before the sandwiches get all dried out and those gulls drive us crazy with their squawking."

The food never tasted better to Wynne. Far on the horizon, they saw a freighter steaming along. Sandpipers ran up and down the edge of the water. The gulls had settled on the sand, all facing them, waiting. Was there bluer sky anywhere? Any more enticing surf? She sighed. Oh, she *had* missed this island! She loved it. Just as it was.

The bridge crossed her mind, the changes it would bring, and she felt sick at heart. She knew why Grandmother felt so strongly about it. She had lived her entire life here. What a heartache it would be to see it all go, to give way to tall hotels and jazzy night spots—all those things tourists demanded. The serenity would end. The privacy would vanish.

They finished eating and fed the gulls the crusts from their sandwiches. Then spreading lotion generously on each other, they stretched out in the sun.

Cheek pressed to the beach towel, Wynne heard the sea singing. She dug her hand into the white sand and let it sift through her fingers. The surf crashed to the beach. And suddenly, even with Lorrie stretched beside her, Wynne felt the music of loneliness moving through her soul. It was so lovely here. So lovely and so lonely.

She turned over on her back to stare at the sky. Then instinctively, she sensed someone near. She turned her head.

The world stopped for a moment. The surf ceased to roll in, and the sky crowded down on her.

"Hello, Wynne," Eric said.

XII

IT WAS an unreal moment for Wynne. Was she awake or dreaming? But as he came toward her, kicking the sand ahead of him, she knew he was real.

"Lorrie, wake up. We've got company."

"What?" Lorrie asked, opening her eyes. "Oh!"

"Such laziness," Eric said lightly. "It's a great day. I'm going to take the boat out. Would the two of you like to come along?"

Lorrie was looking at Wynne, and Wynne stared out to the sea. Eric's boat held memories too. Just as this spot near the lighthouse held memories. Was there any place on the island that didn't remind her of him?

"I'd like to have you," Eric said pointedly.

Wynne was about to decline when Lorrie put a hand on her arm.

"Let's go for a little while," Lorrie said. "It's been a long time since I was out in a boat just for fun."

Wynne still held back. But Eric was already helping Lorrie gather their picnic things. Reluctantly, she folded her beach towel.

"Where would you like to go?" Eric asked.

"Oh, around the island," Lorrie said. "That would be fun, don't you think, Wynne?"

Wynne gave them a stiff smile. "Of course. Anywhere."

This was the last thing in the world she had wanted to happen. But perhaps she couldn't slay the dragon unless she got close enough to see how fierce he really was.

They put the things in the car and drove back to Eric's house. Wynne tried not to remember the many times she had come here. She was anxious to be under way, to have the little jaunt over and done.

It seemed to take Eric a long time. But at last, the

boat was ready, and they eased away from the dock. With his usual zest for speed, Eric opened up the motor, and they skimmed the water. The wind against Wynne's face was cooling and refreshing. Eric handled the boat with skill, and Lorrie seemed bright-eyed and happy. If nothing else, it was worth the trip to see her look this way.

Eric shouted to them over the roar of the motor, pointing to this or that. Incidental things. A new Coast Guard marker. A new slate roof on one of the houses on the island. A condominium at Charlton that rose skyward with its twelve stories.

"Everything's changing," Eric said. "More and more all the time."

The bridge leaped into Wynne's mind. How did Eric feel about it? She didn't really know. The bridge had not been an issue on Feather Island when she had been dating him.

They roared over the water, leaving a foaming wake behind them. Now and then, Eric flung a question in Wynne's direction or gave her a quick look. She was polite, cool. She was content to let Lorrie do most of the talking.

Then at last, Eric put back toward his own dock, and in a few minutes, they had tied up there. Eric gave Lorrie a hand out of the boat and then reached to Wynne.

She hesitated. His eyes flashed.

"It's a big step up, Wynne."

Then his hand gripped hers tightly, and he gave her a little tug up to the dock. For one small moment, he was very close, so close that it would only have taken a slight movement to have gone into his arms. She turned away quickly and walked toward the beach and her car parked just beyond.

"Want to come in?" Eric said. "I'll find something cold to drink."

But Lorrie was taking her cue from Wynne this time and shook her head.

"We'd better get home. It's getting late. Thanks for the ride, Eric."

"Any time," he replied.

"Yes, thank you," Wynne said.

"Oh, by the way, Wynne, I'll be dropping around the hotel one of these days. About your insurance."

She had nearly forgotten that Grandmother carried the insurance with Eric. Well, she would face that when she got to it. Right now, she only wanted to go quickly and not look back.

As they drove back to Lorrie's house, Wynne said little. Lorrie sighed. "Listen, Wynne, you've got to get used to seeing him. You know how it is on Feather Island; everyone sees everyone else."

"I know. I just wasn't ready for it, Lorrie."

"The sooner the better," she pointed out.

"Well, it's over now and no harm done," Wynne said. "You had a good time."

Lorrie nodded. "Yes. It was fun."

"Lorrie, aren't you seeing anyone?"

"No."

"But why not? I'm sure there are lots of men who would find you interesting."

"Who? You know who lives on the island. Not very many eligible bachelors, and besides, Dad scares them all off. The few I know in Charlton don't bother any more."

"That situation is getting a little ridiculous, Lorrie, if you'll pardon my saying so."

"I know. I've just got to bear with it a little while longer."

"Is this what's been bothering you? Is that why you were in tears?" Wynne asked. Then she shook her head. "Listen to me! I was determined not to bring up the subject. It just popped out. Sorry."

Lorrie turned her head and stared out the window. Her hands in her lap were suddenly tense and twisted together.

"I'll just say this much, Wynne. I'm involved in something. Concerning the Hethershaws. I don't know what to do about it."

"I see."

"Please don't ask questions. I just can't discuss it."

"Is there any way I can help?"

Lorrie darted her a brown-eyed look, and Wynne saw

the tears were perilously close. "No. I don't think so. If there ever is a way—"

"I'll be here," Wynne said quietly.

Later, when Wynne reached the South Wind, she parked her car and went into her apartment. She left the picnic things and went out to find Edward.

"I'll watch the desk this evening," Wynne said smiling. "You're due for some time off."

Edward nodded. "Miss Carlson checked in this morning. We've already had a complaint from the Wilkin twins. I've promised you would speak with them."

"What's the problem?"

"Miss Carlson's typewriter. They find it noisy."

Wynne laughed. "I see. Anything else?"

Edward gave her a short smile. "Believe me, that has been enough."

The sun was beginning to drop low in the sky. Wynne went to roll up the bamboo shades in the lobby and let the beauty of the sunset spill into the room. It was a constant battle to keep the lobby windows clear as the moist salty air kept them smudged, but Marge did a good job.

A few clouds scudded across the sun, a small yacht was on the horizon homeward bound, and evening was about to settle down on Feather Island.

"Lovely, isn't it?"

Scott Stoner came to stand beside her.

"Yes. If I had to pick a very favorite spot, I think this would have to be it."

"Would you join me for dinner tonight?"

"I must stay close to the desk."

Scott smiled. He seemed very personable and without sun glasses, she noticed his eyes were hazel, speckled with bits of brown and gold.

"If you won't come to the mountain, the mountain will come to you. Would you join me on the beach at one of the tables there?"

"All right."

"I'll be back in a few minutes."

She went outside. She saw Scott disappearing into the Hurricane and the little dog waiting at the door for him. Wynne sat down at one of the beach tables sheltered by

79

a bright umbrella. She saw the twins coming back from their customary evening stroll.

Nettie saw her at once and came bearing down on her.

"I want to speak with you, Wynne," Nettie said. "It's about that new guest. Diane Carlson. Noisy as they come. Are we going to have to listen to that typewriter of hers going at all hours?"

"I understand Miss Carlson is a writer. She's probably come here to do some work."

"That's beside the point, Wynne," Nettie said. "We're not going to put up with that racket, are we, Lettie?"

Lettie smiled nervously. "Now, Nettie, maybe it's not all that bad—"

"Then you must be losing your hearing!" Nettie snapped. "Well, Wynne—"

"I'll see what can be done," Wynne promised.

"I should hope so!" Nettie said. "This hotel used to be so quiet. So nice. Now, all kinds of people are around. I just don't understand what the world is coming to!"

They walked away at last, and Wynne was relieved. Nettie could wear down anyone's nerves. In a moment, Lettie was back.

"I want you to have this," Lettie said in a whisper.

She pressed a sea shell into Wynne's hand. A perfect whelk.

"But don't you want this for your collection, Lettie?"

"Don't pay any attention to my sister, Wynne. She doesn't really mean to be so cross."

Wynne smiled. She accepted the shell, knowing that Lettie's heart would be broken if she didn't.

"Don't worry about it, Lettie."

Wynne watched the sky, trying not to think about seeing Eric today. She must forget him. It was as simple as that. She must not let her chance encounters with him shake her world.

"Here we are!" Scott said, striding toward her, the little dog at his heels.

He put a tray on the table. It held sandwiches, a pitcher of iced tea, salad, and a special dessert Ruby always served on Sunday.

"Will this do?"

80

"It looks delicious!"

"Ruby found a bone for Mops."

He shook it out of a paper sack and gave it to the little dog.

"Mops?"

Scott laughed. "Yes. I gave him a name. I couldn't just go on calling him 'dog,' now could I? I remember when I was a boy, my mother had the biggest dust mop you ever saw. It and the dog look alike. So—"

Wynne tasted one of the sandwiches.

"Are you a native of Florida, Scott?"

He shook his head. "No. I was born in Wyoming. My parents moved a great deal. I never went to the same school for two years straight. I suppose there is a good side to that too, but I don't know what it is. I've always wanted to put down roots. Deep roots. I think that's a throwback to my grandfather. He was a ranche~ in Wyoming. He wanted nothing else. Just the ranch. A roof over his head. Enough money to get by. His was a simple life."

"It's a simple life here," Wynne pointed out.

Scott smiled. "I've noticed. I like your island, Wynne. I like it very much."

She had no idea who Scott Stoner really was or what he did. She only knew he left the hotel regularly every morning with one of those strange suitcases of his and was gone most of the day.

"You're going to let me take you out for a real dinner sometime, aren't you?"

"But this is very nice, Scott. I'd forgotten how elegant it could be out here," she admitted.

The sea was particularly lovely. The sun was just about to drop out of sight. Everything was taking on a pink hue. They lingered on the beach until it was nearly dark.

They walked back to the hotel, Mops at their heels. Under a palm tree near the front entrance, Scott paused. He reached out and took her by the shoulders. He seemed very tall, very attentive, very attractive in the half-light.

"Good-night, Wynne."

He kissed her. She was startled and yet did nothing

to stop him. His lips were warm and hungry. It was pleasant. But no more. He sensed this.

"Someday, Wynne Russell, you're going to kiss me the way I want you to kiss me!"

XIII

SCOTT DISAPPEARED up the steps to his room as Wynne went to answer the desk phone.

"South Wind Hotel."

"Edward Allen, please."

"One moment. I'll ring his room."

She rang Edward's room several times, but there was no answer.

"I'm sorry, Mr. Allen seems to be out. May I take a message?"

There was no reply. Just a sudden click on the end of the line. Wynne frowned. Who had it been? A soft, feminine voice. One she should recognize, but for the life of her, she couldn't put a name to it. The call surprised her. Edward seemed to have no friends. She had no idea what he did with his spare time, but she seldom saw him fishing or swimming. In fact, she knew very little about Edward Allen.

The next morning, Wynne was at the desk when she looked up to find Sam coming into the hotel with his rolling gait. Usually, she went down to the post office to collect the mail, but she saw that Sam had saved her the bother today.

"Are you back from Charlton so early?"

"I'm ahead of schedule for a change. I thought you'd like to have this, so I fetched it up."

He put the mail on the top of the desk, and she saw the letter on top.

"It's from Dad! Bless you, Sam. I've been so anxious to hear."

The note was full of news. He was in Miami but planning a tour of the Western states. He seemed relaxed and happy. But as Wynne read further, she sensed he might be a little uncomfortable in his new role of a man of leisure. Could it be that he missed the South Wind after all? Or was it the quarrel with his mother that nettled him?

"How is he?" Sam asked. "What's he got to say?"

"Nothing very much. But he's fine, Sam. He didn't mention Grandmother."

"Give him time. He'll come around."

"Perhaps," she replied. "But will Grandmother?"

That was another story, and they both knew it. Grandmother had a will of iron.

"One more thing of interest," Captain Sam said. "This one will really open your eyes. Everybody on the island got one. Even Will Dykes."

It was an engraved invitation. Very fancy. Very formal.

"From Max and Ilsa Hethershaw!" Wynne said with surprise.

"They're having open house. A party. For everybody on the island. Now, can you figure that one?"

Wynne shook her head. "No, I can't."

"I can't either. Nobody was ever invited up there before."

Wynne reread the invitation. It did seem strange, and yet the prospect of going there was rather interesting. She had been in the house just once. But it had lingered in her mind. It had always been the talk of Feather Island. Just as Max and Ilsa were the main topics of gossip.

"You will go, won't you, Sam?" Wynne asked.

Sam shrugged. "Oh, I may dust off my best suit and give it a whirl, just to see what Max has got up his sleeve."

Later, she got quite a different reaction from Grandmother.

"I most certainly will *not* go! Max Hethershaw! He wants the bridge, of course. Everyone knows that. It will mean more money in his pocket."

"Don't you want to be neighborly?"

"Neighborly!" Grandmother scoffed. "He doesn't know the meaning of the word."

"I'm going," Wynne said with a lift of her chin.

Grandmother glared at her, pursed her lips, and said

nothing. But she didn't like it, and Wynne knew that for days the old lady would be angry about it.

The party was soon the talk of the island. Wynne heard about it wherever she went. No one could understand why Hethershaw had decided to host them all. Many thought it was more than likely Ilsa's doing. The island was sharply divided. Some would not go. Others couldn't wait.

A few days later, Wynne decided to take the ferry to Charlton and do some shopping. She needed a new party dress, and she had been concentrating so hard on running the South Wind that it would be good to get away. She had managed to get permission from Grandmother to make the necessary repairs. Other things were still pending. Wynne had a sinking feeling that Grandmother would never agree to them. All she could do was her best with what she had.

Charlton was a busy city, and it brought back memories of Tallahassee and Jack Brown. She missed her work there, and yet she knew every day she spent at the South Wind, she loved the old hotel a little bit more.

She took the regular five o'clock ferry back to Feather Island, her car loaded with packages. When she stepped out of her car, she saw Sam motioning to her wildly. She joined him at the wheel. She could tell from the very way he bit down on his pipe that something had happened.

"They're here," Sam said.

"Who?"

"The survey crew! I took them over about noon. Had a call to come and get them. They've got a couple of trucks and a load of equipment. Four men."

There was a sinking sensation in the pit of Wynne's stomach.

"Does that mean—"

"Doesn't mean a thing!" Sam said firmly. "It's not too late to kill it. Has your grandmother heard anything from Tallahassee?"

"Not a word," Wynne admitted.

They stood silently together, contemplating what this meant. Wynne tried to imagine how it would look with a bridge stretched across to the island, with streams of cars bringing new people. Now, with the island accessible only by ferry, tourists simply found it not worth the bother to visit. The bridge would quickly change all of that.

"I hear there's a bunch of businessmen in Charlton who have formed a committee. They're doing everything they can to get the bridge," Sam said.

"It figures," Wynne nodded.

"Only one of them isn't from Charlton," Sam said quietly. "He's from the island."

Wynne stared at him. Sam was suddenly very busy handling the ferry.

"You mean Eric, don't you? He's the only businessman I know from Feather Island that works at Charlton."

"Just a guess, Wynne. Sorry. Hate to say it, but I'm afraid Eric's on the other side of the fence."

Wynne sighed. "Well, he has been for a long time for me, Sam."

When she reached the island, she drove off the ferry and went straight to the hotel. She couldn't get out of her mind what Sam had hinted about Eric. He used to love the island just as it was. Had he changed so much? Yes, perhaps he had. She no longer knew him.

She relieved Edward at the desk, and he went next door to have his evening meal. It was a short time later that she heard the slamming of car doors and looked up to find four men striding into the hotel lobby.

"Good evening," she said. "May I help you?"

"We'd like four rooms."

They wore work clothes and had rolls of maps under their arms. She knew instantly who they were, but she had not expected them to come here.

"We'll be here a couple of weeks, miss."

She swallowed hard. She badly needed to rent the four rooms. But this was the enemy.

"Well?" the man said. "Don't you have accommodations?"

She made up her mind in an instant. She turned the register for them to sign their names and plucked four keys down from their hooks.

In a few moments, they had stamped their way up the steps and disappeared, talking among themselves.

Wynne experienced an instant headache. It wouldn't take long for the islanders to find out they were staying here. Word would spread like wildfire.

A few moments later, Scott came into the lobby and paused at the desk.

"How would you like to go to Charlton tonight? I've heard of a new place. Pirate's Roost. It sounds like fun."

Scott was watching her closely. He seemed so eager for her to accept. She was rather intrigued with this man. She had not forgotten the kiss he had given her or the promise. She was more than a little curious about him.

"All right, Scott, I'd like to go."

She stayed at the desk until Edward came back. It was normally his night off, but she tried to press him into service.

"I'm sorry, Miss Russell. I've already made plans."

"Well then, I'll see if George Laughlin will fill in."

When George was asked, he was pleased to help.

"I don't know what I'd do without you, George," Wynne told him.

"I want to know who owns those trucks," George said.

"Four men from the highway commission," she answered.

George lifted his brows. When Wynne left him at the desk, she saw him pick up the phone to spread the word.

Wynne was nearly dressed when her phone rang. She wasn't really surprised to hear Grandmother's voice on the other end of the line.

"I want to see you. Right away," Grandmother said.

"I have a date this evening."

"Cancel it. I must talk with you."

The line went dead. Wynne was seething with quick anger as she hung up. Her headache was getting no better. She phoned Scott's room and told him what had happened.

"No problem," he said. "I'll drive you there and wait while you talk with her."

His voice was so warm, so kind. She felt a little ripple of response. Then it was immediately gone as she wondered about the meeting with Grandmother.

A short time later, just as the sun was edging downward to the water on the horizon, Scott drove her to her grandmother's house. She invited him in to meet the old lady, but he declined.

"Not this time. I'm sure you have business to discuss. I'll wait here."

She left him leaning against the fender of his car. Mops went everywhere with him, and Scott let the dog out of the car to exercise. She saw them strike off toward the beach as she lifted the knocker on the door.

Grandmother was watching the sunset. If she saw Scott and Mops, she made no mention of them. She came right to the point.

"Is it true that those survey men are staying at the hotel?"

"Yes."

"Get them out!"

Wynne knotted her fists. "No, Grandmother. They're staying. They've taken the rooms for two weeks, and they've paid in advance."

"I want them out."

"We're in the hotel business. We rent to anyone who pays his bills and is decent and respectable. Unless they create too much noise or become some kind of nuisance, they stay."

Grandmother got to her feet. She eyed Wynne with her bright blue eyes. "They are here to bring the bridge! How dare you rent to them!"

"If you want them out, Grandmother, you'll have to do it yourself."

With that, Wynne turned on her heel and walked out of the room, her cheeks flushed, her hands cold. It was the first real disagreement they'd had. It had to come sometime, she supposed.

She went down to the beach. Scott saw her and came to meet her.

"Ready so soon?" he asked.

Then he saw how he looked, and he put out a hand to touch her cheek. "Want to tell me what happened?"

"No."

"You're not going to cry!"

"If I do it's only because I'm so darned mad!" she burst out.

Scott put an arm around her shoulder, whistled to Mops, and they began walking along the beach toward the house and the car.

"I've heard about your grandmother," Scott said.

"Everyone on the island has," Wynne replied.

"But I have a feeling, Wynne, that you're going to prove to be a match for her."

"Oh, sometimes, I wish I had never come back here. I wish I had never been so softhearted. Everything's just in one big mess!"

"But if you hadn't come, I wouldn't have met you," Scott said warmly. "And I think that would have been the biggest tragedy of my life."

He paused and turned her to him. He lifted her chin and smiled at her.

"Now, shall we go to dinner? For a little while, forget about bridges and hotels and islands," he said. "Think about having a good time."

She began to relax. He had that effect on her. Whenever she was with him, she found herself letting down.

"One more thing," he said. "Think about me."

XIV

Scott drove down to Captain Sam's dock.

"I've arranged to rent one of his small boats. If you'll trust me at the helm."

Captain Sam came out and stood there for a moment, looking at them. He was angry about something. Wynne knew all the signs. And she knew what he was angry about. He had heard about the survey crew. Her heart did another flip-flop. She knew how strongly he felt about the bridge. But somehow, she had not expected him to take this stand.

"I'll leave the dock light on," Sam said sourly. "If I'm not up when you come back, just tie it up and drop the keys in my mail box."

If Scott noticed Sam's coolness, he didn't say anything about it. They left Mops in the car, and he barked woefully to them as they boarded the boat and moved away. Scott handled the boat in a steady, sure way. She sensed that everything about Scott was steady and sure.

She was determined to have a good time tonight. She wanted desperately to forget everything. All the problems, her grandmother's wrath and her own uncertainty about whether she'd done right or not.

The night air felt cool against Wynne's flushed cheeks. Soon, they were nearing the lights of Charlton, and Scott tied up the boat. A few minutes later, a cab came to take them to the Pirate's Roost. It was an amusing place. Very dark and secluded, with waiters dressed in pirate costumes. A few wore dark patches over their eyes, and the wall was decorated with huge knives and swords.

"Blackbeard should walk in any minute," Scott laughed.

"Perhaps I should open a place like this in my hotel," Wynne said.

Scott toyed with the silverware. He had such interesting hands. Long-fingered, slender, but very strong.

"You came to take over when your father left, is that it?"

"You've been listening to the gossips," Wynne smiled.

"There's been some talk around. I don't pay much attention to it. You came to help your grandmother out of a jam."

"She had no one else."

Scott gave her a warm smile. "I find that interesting. You're compassionate."

"And perhaps very foolish. After tonight, I'm not at all sure I should stay."

"You're not the sort that runs away from trouble. I'd bet on it," Scott said.

"Enough about me. Tell me more about you."

"Not much to tell."

"I know a little about your background. Not much else."

"I'm here on a job, Wynne. I can't tell you more than that."

She gave a startled gasp. "The bridge! You've got something to do—"

He laughed and reached out to cover her hand with his.

"Thank God, no, it's not the bridge. If it were, I don't think you'd even associate with me. Do you hate the idea so much?"

"It will ruin things, Scott. It will probably put the South Wind out of business. Grandmother knows it too, although she never says so in so many words. But it's there, like some dark cloud hanging over our heads."

"I take it the hotel has always been in the family?"

"Yes. From the very beginning. My grandfather built it. Years and years ago. Grandmother managed it alone after he died a long time ago. Then, when she felt she was too old to continue taking care of it, my father was pressed into service."

"And now you."

"When Dad took over, I was eleven years old. Impressionable. I fell in love with Feather Island and the old hotel. Most of the important things in my life have happened there. Do you understand?"

91

"I envy you," Scott said. "I've never been in one place long enough to call it home. And that's what you're calling the South Wind. Home."

"Yes. But there's another side too, Scott. Call it pride. Or integrity. The South Wind stood for something. I want it to always stand for something. The Russells can be very stubborn. We don't like to give up."

They enjoyed the food and the atmosphere. Somehow, Scott made her feel easier about the whole business of giving shelter to the enemy. They lingered for a long while at the Pirate's Roost.

"Scott, I know this is going to sound strange, but I keep thinking I'd seen you before you came to Feather Island."

He gave her a long look. "Do you?"

"Have I? Could I have met you in Tallahassee or was it Miami?"

"We haven't met before, Wynne. I wish we had."

She saw the light deepen in his eyes. She looked away, uncertain and confused. She found with surprise that she wanted to respond to Scott's warmth. It was an odd feeling. For so long, she had thought only of Eric and her pain at losing him.

They left the Pirate's Roost at last, and Scott suggested a short walk.

"There's a little store a few blocks away that stays open all night. I want to get something."

The little store handled a variety of things. But she saw at once what it was he wanted. He spent nearly ten minutes examining every dog collar they had and finally selected one that was bright red and trimmed with silver metal.

"For Mops," he said. "If he's my dog, I want him to have a collar and a tag. I'll pick up the license for him the first chance I get."

A cab took them back to the dock. Scott helped her into the boat, and soon they were headed back to Feather Island. The stars were bright and thick in the sky overhead. The water made soft slushing sounds against the bow. Captain Sam's dock light was a beacon in the darkness.

The wind against Wynne's face seemed warm and sweet.

"It's a beautiful night. It's a great little island, Wynne. I can see why you love it so much."

When they reached the dock, Captain Sam's little office was dark. Mops barked his greeting as Scott dropped the key into the mail box.

Before they drove away, Scott took the dog collar out of the paper sack and fastened it around Mops's neck. Mops shook himself a few times and barked.

"Sh! You'll wake up Sam," Scott laughed. "He looks real fancy, doesn't he, Wynne?"

"He belongs to you now."

The drive back to the hotel took but a few minutes, but Scott was in no hurry. He took her on past the South Wind.

"I've been hearing about Sunset Point. I'd like to see it."

"It's on private property."

"Then let them chase us away, if they want to."

Sunset Point was truly one of the loveliest spots on the island. It had been a long time since Wynne had visited it. Mostly because it was on Hethershaw's land, and visitors weren't encouraged. Now, with the moon just coming, it showed the water and the treacherous rocks below. She thought about Brad diving there and shuddered. He'd better forget the entire idea!

"They tell me the water is very deep down there," Scott said.

"Yes."

"A lovely place but dangerous too. Like most women."

"Why, Scott, what a terrible thing to say!"

Scott laughed softly. "It's true. A woman can be lovely and dangerous all at the same time. A threat. Like the bridge is a threat to the island's serenity."

"What kind of women have you known?" she asked lightly.

"Not many," he admitted. "None as lovely as you. You're the first redhead I ever knew. I have a feeling you could be very dangerous."

He reached out for her then. She found herself willingly being swept into his arms.

93

"I thought so," Scott said. "I think I've just taken a step over that cliff, and I'm falling."

She didn't know what to say.

"Would you believe me if I told you I had never done anything like this before?" he asked.

She decided to treat the whole matter lightly.

"It's called island madness. We all get it in one form or another."

"If this is madness, I like it."

She moved away to wrap her arm around a palm that grew at the very edge of the cliff. She clung to it, needing the feel of something solid. What kind of hypnotism did this man practice? She felt unreasonably lightheaded, giddy.

At last they drove back to the hotel, down the quiet road, and past the sleeping houses. The lights in the hotel lobby had been dimmed. George had gone to bed. As they stepped across the veranda, Scott paused.

"I intend to see you again, Wynne."

"Danger and all?" she laughed.

"Danger and all," he said.

She watched him go up the steps to his room. Then she stepped around behind the desk to take a quick look at things. Everything seemed in order. The hotel was quiet. Then as she went through the office into her apartment, she spied the envelope. Her name was typed across it. With a puzzled frown, she opened it and saw that it was from Lorrie.

Meet me at Two Palms as soon as you can. I'll wait. Urgent.

Wynne stared at the note, a kind of nameless fear creeping over her. She had been worried about Lorrie. She knew something was very wrong in her friend's life. Now, to receive this mysterious note—

She snatched up her purse, searched it for her car keys, and left the hotel quickly. Two Palms was about a mile from the hotel, a wooded picnic area where they had often visited as young girls. It was marked by two distinctive palm trees. The rest were mangrove and pine.

The night seemed black now. Even though the stars were still shining. Without Scott beside her, she felt alone and uneasy.

She drove slowly as the roads wouldn't let her go very fast, and somehow, it seemed her car was very noisy in the dead of the night.

When she reached Two Palms, she turned in and immediately clicked off the lights. She waited for a moment, looking around. The area seemed deserted. If Lorrie was here, why didn't she come forward?

Slowly, Wynne opened the car door. She climbed out, uncertain, a little afraid.

"Lorrie, where are you?"

There was no reply. She began walking toward the sea, passing the picnic tables, and emerging at last to the white beach. She had stepped into some kind of burrs, and she felt them sticking through her hose. She picked them off, stuck her fingers until one of them bled, and still, she could see no sign of Lorrie. Perhaps she had grown tried of waiting and had simply gone home. Yes, that was surely it.

She would go back to the car. Drive to Lorrie's house. Awaken her if necessary. But right now, she wanted to get out of here. Fast!

It was then she spied something caught in the rocks on the beach. She bent to retrieve it and felt the soft material under her fingers. A scarf? She went back to the car. There, in the lights from the dashboard, she saw the scarf was very bright, probably very expensive.

The kind Ilsa would wear. Perhaps she had lost it here one day. She would see about returning it tomorrow.

She drove fast now, stirring the dust behind her, and it seemed to take a very long time to reach Lorrie's house. All was dark, quiet. She hesitated. Perhaps the note hadn't been as important as it seemed. Perhaps the thing to do was simply turn around and wait until tomorrow.

No. She couldn't. She wouldn't sleep a wink if she did that. She walked quickly to the house and around to the side window that opened into Lorrie's room.

"Lorrie," she called softly. "Lorrie, it's me, Wynne. Come out, will you?"

There was no reply. She picked up a handful of pebbles and tossed them against the window. They echoed loudly in the still night. But there was no reply, no light coming on.

She was frightened now. Where was Lorrie? The door opened. Will stood there.

"What's goin' on?" Will demanded. "What are you doing here, Wynne?"

"I want to see Lorrie," she explained.

"Lorrie ain't here. She's up to the house on the hill. Staying over nights now. Helping them get ready for that big party."

Full of apologies she hurried away. She wouldn't go up to the Hethershaw place at this time of night. Nor could she phone. She sensed Lorrie would not like that. She had been so secretive about it all.

No, all she could do now was wait until tomorrow. She would ask Lorrie about the note then.

XV

THE WILKIN TWINS were clearly excited about attending the Hethershaw party. Because they were, George Laughlin decided immediately that he would not go. Wynne smiled at their little game of war. But she felt sorry for the three of them. What excitement did they have but these bickering quarrels?

There was no word from Grandmother, but she had not expected any. When evening came, Wynne put on her new party dress, brushed her red hair until it shone, and went out to the lobby. The twins had asked her to drive them up to the house on the hill, and Scott, who was surprised at also being invited, had promised to take them all.

They met in the lobby and were soon on their way. Several other cars were on the road, all heading to the Hethershaw mansion.

The place was ablaze with lights. Coming to it as they did just at twilight, it took on a different look, perhaps even more elegant than it actually was.

Car doors slammed. Voices echoed. Everyone exchanged nervous smiles. Then the door was open and Max Hethershaw stood there, his graying hair neatly combed, his clothes well tailored, giving him a look of fashion and authority.

He shook hands with them all. He welcomed them with a bright smile. Was it a real smile or a false one? The man seemed nervous. When Wynne shook hands with him, she saw the little beads of perspiration above his lips.

"Hello, Max."

"Wynne," he nodded. "Nice seeing you again."

"But where is Ilsa?"

A blank look came to his eyes. His lips twitched. "I'm sorry. It was quite unexpected. She had to leave the island for a few days. Rather than change plans for the party, she insisted I go ahead without her."

Wynne was startled. Ilsa Hethershaw would have gloried in such an evening as this!

"I hope it wasn't anything too terrible. Emergencies have a way of scaring a person to death."

"Illness in her family. You understand—"

"Of course. But I'm sorry that she's not able to be here."

Max took a handkerchief from his pocket and dabbed at his forehead. "Please enjoy yourself, Wynne. My house is yours."

She moved away from him, still carrying the silk scarf she had found last night, which she had intended to ask Ilsa about.

Scott joined a group of men, and Wynne looked for Lorrie. But she was nowhere in sight. Mattie was passing a large tray of hors d'oeuvres. Then Wynne saw Brad bearing down on her.

"Have you seen the view from the balcony?"

"No."

"Then you must. Come along. It's stupendous. And wait until you see the water down there!"

The balcony offered a view like no one else on the island had. Not even Grandmother. The breeze was soft, caressing. Wynne gripped the railing and looked down to the water. It was immediately below. Why had Max built the balcony like this? It was dangerous. What if someone fell over the railing? They would be dashed to death on the rocks below, or if not that, surely drowned in the churning, treacherous water.

"Isn't it great?" Brad asked.

"It frightens me."

Brad dropped an arm around her shoulders. "Look that way. See the evening star? I never realized before that you could see down to Dolphin Bay from here. I must come up here and dive. I never did bring my boat right into the bay. But tomorrow—I think I will!"

"I wish you wouldn't, Brad."

"Why?" he asked with a laugh. "This will more than likely prove to be a diver's paradise!"

"Call it a premonition, if you will. I just have this awful feeling that you shouldn't."

There were a great many people crowded into Max's house. Max was talking with the Wilkin twins, and plainly, they were being charmed right out of their shoes. Wynne smiled to herself. The old girls would have something to talk about for days.

There was music, and out on the brick terrace to the right of the house, a few were dancing.

"Let's join them," Brad said.

She looked for Scott, but couldn't see him in the crowd. Brad held her close as they danced. Japanese lanterns swung in the breeze. Everyone was wearing party clothes. The champagne was flowing. Max had really put himself out for this party and still it nagged at Wynne. Why?

"Wynne, I've been thinking," Brad said. "Why don't you come to North Dakota this winter! See all that snow."

"And leave the sunny shores of Feather Island?" she laughed. "I'd have to be crazy."

"I'd like to show you my country. You have any idea how cozy a winter night can be with a fire roaring in the fireplace, with the snow falling outside the window?"

"No."

"Come to North Dakota next winter, and I'll show you."

Brad leaned toward her. With surprise, she saw he intended to kiss her. She turned her cheek quickly.

"Don't, Brad."

"Why not?"

"Please, just don't."

"It's Eric Channon, isn't it?"

She missed a step. "What do you know about Eric?"

"I've heard. Lots of things."

Brad moved her easily over the terrace floor. Then, with a kind of relief, she saw Scott. He came to put a hand on Brad's shoulders.

"May I have a turn with the lady?"

He didn't give Brad a chance to answer. Instead, he

simply pulled Wynne into his arms and danced her away. But in a moment, Scott had stopped dancing and tugged her from the terrace and the bright lights. There was a garden here. Roses were blooming. On a stone bench, Scott pulled her down beside him.

"I'm not much for dancing, do you mind?"

"No."

"Was that a 'come rescue me look' you gave me just now?"

She laughed. "Yes. Thank you."

"What is Eric Channon to you?"

She swallowed hard.

"I couldn't help overhearing," he said.

"Eric is someone I want to forget," she said quickly. "I don't care to discuss him."

They grew quiet for a little while. Then Scott changed the subject.

"Who's minding the hotel?" he asked.

"George Laughlin. He didn't care to come to the party. So that freed both Edward and myself."

"But Edward's not here. I saw him leaving on the ferry late this afternoon."

"I sometimes think Edward has a big romance going on somewhere," Wynne smiled. "But you'd never know it. He never talks about it. He's a very strange and remote young man. But he does his work well enough."

After a time, they went back inside to the bright lights and music. The room was crowded. It would seem that Max's party had overcome some of the more hostile people on the island. Curiosity was a great enticer. Benson, for one, was there. He was nervously smoking a cigar. The Ward brothers were present too. And Ruby Hammer. Captain Sam was absent. Wynne was sorry and disappointed. Somehow, she had hoped to ease the situation between them. It nagged at her that he was angry with her. When had Sam ever been angry with her before?

Then she was suddenly aware that others were angry too. She was being given the cool treatment by nearly everyone. Her smiles or nods were either frowned upon or ignored completely. Her pulse began to leap in her throat. They were *all* against her!

Ruby Hammer came to speak with her. "You're getting the ice too, I see."

"You mean you—"

"I've been feeding the survey crew, you've been housing them. In their twisted little minds, that makes us one of them."

"Oh, dear!" Wynne sighed. "I didn't know what else to do, Ruby."

"It's hard for me to turn away a hungry man," Ruby said. "Even surveyors!"

Benson, the grocer, was beginning to talk very loudly to the Ward brothers.

"The bridge is no damned good! A cock-eyed idea, meant to put money in the pockets of certain people we all know! Some are already cashing in."

The room grew very still. Wynne's cheeks flushed. They were looking at her and Ruby. Then she became aware of Max. He stood very straight, very cold, looking at Benson with a glare that would have wilted almost anyone. Tension crackled in the room.

Wynne felt as if she were responsible, at least in part. But what could she do? She groped in her purse for the silk scarf she had found last night on the beach.

"Oh, Max, could I speak with you for a moment, please?" Wynne asked. "I think this belongs to Ilsa."

Max grew tense at the sight of the scarf. He took it from her hand and fingered it.

"Would you come into the library, Wynne? I'd like to speak to you about this."

Everyone began murmuring again. The crisis had been averted. Wynne followed Max into the quiet library. It was an impressive place with rows and rows of books from the ceiling to the floor. A huge desk commanded the center of the room. She imagined this was where Lorrie did her work.

"I'm sure it is Ilsa's," Max began. "I gave it to her only a few days ago. Tell me, where did you find it?"

"On the beach."

He turned sharply to stare at her. "Where on the beach? It's important."

"Why, near Two Palms."

"When did you find it?"

"Last night."

Max reached up to rub his mustache and nodded. "Thank you. I'll put it away for safe keeping."

He opened a desk drawer and tucked it inside. He seemed shaken. She couldn't imagine why. All because Ilsa had lost an expensive scarf? With all the money Max Hethershaw had, what was one small scarf?

"Now, if you'll excuse me, I must get back to my guests."

"Max, is Lorrie here? I want to see her."

He nodded. "She's helping in the kitchen. Mattie's had her hands full with the party."

Wynne located the kitchen and stepped through the swinging doors. Trays of food were still much in evidence, and the champagne glasses were still being filled.

"Lorrie!"

Lorrie looked up, startled.

"What are you doing in here, Lorrie? Aren't you going to join the party?"

"I promised I'd help Mattie."

"Can't we talk?"

Lorrie gave her a quick, brown-eyed look and nodded.

"I'm listening."

"Why did you leave that note and then not meet me?"

Lorrie stared at her. "I don't know what you're talking about."

Wynne explained, and the more she talked the more alarmed Lorrie became.

"But I never wrote you a note!" Lorrie exclaimed. "I haven't been away from this house for several days."

"But why would someone—I don't understand."

"Two Palms, did you say?" Lorrie asked, and there was a bright light in her eyes.

"Yes!"

"That's where Ilsa went so often. I think that's where she was meeting him—"

Wynne shook her head. "I don't understand. How did Ilsa get into this. I did find her scarf there. I gave it to Max."

"You gave it to Max! Did you tell him where you found it?"

"Of course. Lorrie, what's going on around here?"

102

Lorrie licked her lips. "I can't tell you. I must not tell you. If Max ever found out I knew anything—"

Lorrie had gone pasty white, and she looked terrified. "You don't know him, Wynne. You don't know what he's really like—"

"Lorrie, you're not making any sense! Now what is it?"

Lorrie moved to the kitchen door and peered out. Then she came back. She gripped Wynne's arm with icy fingers.

"Wynne, I don't think Ilsa got called away on an emergency. I think that's just a story Max made up. I haven't seen Ilsa since yesterday morning, but her clothes are all in her room. There isn't a piece of luggage missing. She's simply disappeared!"

XVI

MATTIE CAME BACK into the room, carrying an empty tray. She was never very communicative. Now, she glared at Wynne with an expression that clearly said Wynne was not wanted or needed in her kitchen.

Wynne gripped Lorrie's hand for a moment. It was still ice-cold. But they couldn't talk now. She could only give Lorrie a smile and walk away. But her thoughts were reeling. Perhaps this explained why Max had become so excited about Ilsa's scarf, and why he had been so insistent upon knowing where it had been found. Lorrie had implied that Ilsa was meeting someone. Another man? It wouldn't be hard to believe. Ilsa was so young, so full of life, so beautiful. A man like Max Hethershaw had a great deal to offer. Money, position, good looks. But he was much older than Ilsa. He was often gone from the island all day. Ilsa had struck her as being a very lonely and perhaps unhappy young woman.

Scott was waiting for her.

"Benson has gone," Scott said. "I don't think there will be any more incidents."

"I think the party is over," Wynne said. "Several are leaving. I think the twins are ready too."

Wynne found that she was suddenly very anxious to leave this fancy house on the hill and the ominous presence of Max Hethershaw. But she hated leaving Lorrie here.

They shook hands with Max and said good-night, thanking him for the party. At last, they were free to go. All the way down the hill, the twins couldn't stop talking about the party, and they were still chatting eagerly about the evening when they reached the hotel and hurried away to their suite.

"Let's take a walk," Scott said. "Along the beach."

The surf glinted in the starlight. Everything seemed so serene, quiet, lovely. Could Lorrie be wrong or had Ilsa Hethershaw truly disappeared?

"You're very quiet," Scott said.

"Did you enjoy the party?"

"Yes. But I was sorry not to meet Ilsa Hethershaw. I've heard so much about her."

"Should I be jealous?" she teased.

Scott stopped walking. He pulled her close. For a long moment, he kissed her recklessly, hungrily, until she broke away with a laugh.

"All right, I shouldn't be jealous," she said.

They weren't far from the South Wind. Suddenly the peaceful night was shattered with the sound of breaking glass.

"What was that?" she gasped.

"The hotel!" Scott said. "It's the hotel—"

They ran. Never had Wynne moved so fast. The air was stinging her lungs, and her throat was aching with a dry nameless terror. When they reached the hotel, she saw the shattered glass. The large front window of the lobby had been broken. They rushed inside. Some of the guests had heard the commotion and came down to investigate. The twins had not yet retired and they stood there, wide-eyed with wonder, staring at the broken window.

Scott bent down and picked up a large stone. "Someone must have pitched it right through the glass. It was no accident, Wynne. Somebody meant to do this!"

"But why?" Nettie asked indignantly. "Why would anyone want to do that?"

"Politics," George Laughlin said, appearing in a robe. "Island politics."

Two of the survey crew had also come down to see what was wrong. It was Nettie who put it into terse words.

"It happened because of you!" Nettie said, pointing at the men. "Because *you're* staying here."

The two men looked uneasy. They did the only sensible thing they could do, turned on their heels and went back to their rooms.

"Nettie, you shouldn't have said that," Wynne said.

"But it's the truth!" Nettie said with a sniff. "Everyone is talking about it. The whole island."

"And tonight someone decided to protest in earnest," Scott said with a frown.

Scott went to find a broom in the supply room. Wynne persuaded everyone to go back to their rooms. Scott finished getting the last of the glass off the lobby floor.

"I'd better try and patch this window someway, Wynne. If you've got some wood or heavy cardboard, I'll see what I can do."

"Perhaps in the supply room."

In a few minutes, Ruby Hammer arrived. She looked at the shattered window with worried eyes. "So, it's started! I suppose my place will be next."

"I just can't believe this has happened."

"Don't forget to phone Eric, Wynne. The insurance should handle this," Ruby said.

She hadn't thought about insurance. Or Eric. She didn't welcome the encounter, but the new window would be costly. She would make an insurance claim.

But worst of all, how was she going to tell Grandmother about this? This would only add fuel to the fire that was already raging between them.

Wynne's head was aching when she finally thanked Scott for his help and went to her apartment. She had one crazy idea of packing up and leaving. Of going back to Tallahassee. Dad had been smart in getting out when he did. But she was caught here, and she knew it. In the first place, it had been a matter of pride. Now, it was more. It was hardheaded stubbornness. She wouldn't let them run her out. No matter how many stones they tossed through the windows!

Max Hethershaw had stayed in his room late the morning after the party. He had not slept all night. In the other room, he could hear Mattie clearing away the party things and Lorrie's quiet voice. He pulled on a robe and went to the den. There in the desk, he took out the silk scarf Wynne Russell had returned to him last night. She had found it at Two Palms, the place where Will

Dykes had seen Ilsa with—who? That was the question. Who? It was driving him mad, wanting to know.

Then yesterday morning, Ilsa had left the house. She'd been wearing this scarf with a bright blouse. Sunglasses. Sandals. She'd had her white purse with her.

When she did not come home for lunch or dinner, he discreetly made a few phone calls. Night came and still she had not returned. He got in his car and drove around, looking for her. Her red car was not in the garage. Although she had not driven it in days, fearing it would break down as Will Dykes had warned her, it was gone. He had put a call in to Hoffman yesterday and been unable to reach him.

Somehow, someway, like a robot, he had got through the nightmarish party, he had smiled and made small talk and acted the part of the charming host to the hilt. Lorrie and Mattie had been told no different. They thought Ilsa had gone—on an emergency, just as he had said. But how much longer could he keep the truth from them? Mattie he could trust. He didn't know about Lorrie.

He reached for the phone and put another call in to Hoffman. The rain was just starting outside the window. Hoffman took a long time to answer.

"This is Max Hethershaw."

"Good morning, sir."

"I want you here. As soon as possible."

Max paced the floor while he waited. A short squall came up, pounding the rain against the house. Mattie knocked at the door.

"Breakfast, Mr. Hethershaw?"

"No. I don't want anything. Is Lorrie out there?"

"Yes."

"Send her in."

Lorrie Dykes was a pretty young woman. He'd found her competent and hard working. Quite different from her father. He'd been prepared to dislike the girl, considering the conditions under which he had hired her. But that was beside the point now. He was certain the girl knew nothing about her father's underhanded ways or why he had hired her in the first place. It had all been a mistake. Letting a man like Will Dykes get any kind of a hold on him was ridiculous. But on the other hand, what could he do? Will knew something about Ilsa. Ilsa and the other man. Hiring Lorrie to keep Will's mouth shut had been worth every penny it had cost him.

"What is it, Mr. Hethershaw?" Lorrie asked.

"With Ilsa away for a few days, I don't think it will be necessary for you to stay here."

"I understand." The girl seemed immensely relieved.

"You've been a great help to me, and when Ilsa returns, we'll get in touch."

"Thank you, sir."

"There's one thing you might do. Go down and fetch the mail."

"Yes, sir."

"Use my car," he said. "Get back as quickly as you can."

Lorrie left, the keys in her hand. Max paced about. When he knew Mattie was busy in the kitchen, he went into Ilsa's room. Methodically, he searched her closets. Her things were all accounted for. This was what puzzled him. Ilsa loved every stitch in this closet. Always wanted more and more. The expensive luggage he had given her last year was all there too. Nothing was missing. Only the clothes she had worn and her red car were gone.

What was keeping Hoffman? The clouds had blown away. The sun was out. Max heard the car coming up the drive. Lorrie was back. She brought in the mail and put it on the desk in front of him.

"I'll be leaving now."

He scarcely heard her. She left in such a rush that she nearly stumbled through the door. He checked the *Wall Street Journal* first. His usual custom. Then as he started sorting through the letters, he heard the boat. Hoffman had arrived. He left by way of the terrace and took the steps down to the dock.

Hoffman got out, briefcase in his hand.

"I must say this is quite different from the way I came the first time," Hoffman said drily.

The man was being cheeky. Max bristled. "I had my reasons. I explained to you that I didn't want my wife to know I was hiring you. I didn't want anyone in Charlton to know it either. That's beside the point. I want a report, and I want it now. What have you found out about my wife?"

Hoffman shook his head. "You might as well have saved your money. She's clean. I couldn't find a thing. She's been seen nowhere in Charlton with another man."

"And here on the island?"

"No. Not as far as I can determine. Investigating on Feather Island is tricky, but I do have a reliable source, Mr. Hethershaw."

Max felt as if someone had knocked the wind out of him. He was stunned with relief.

"You're positive?"

"I'd stake my reputation on it, Mr. Hethershaw. If there's another man in your wife's life, he's surely invisible."

Max nodded. "Send me your bill. Your services are no longer needed. Thank you."

Hoffman grinned and shook his hand and climbed back into the boat. The idea of hiring a private detective had been distasteful to Max. But it had been Ilsa herself who had given him the idea. Thank God, his suspicions had been unfounded.

But still there was the question, where was Ilsa? Had something happened to her? An accident? Soon he would be forced to tell the police about her disappearance. He would have to explain his delay in contacting them, and it might get sticky.

He returned to his den. He dreaded phoning the police. Perhaps he would wait. He began sorting the mail. Had she simply grown tired of him? She had been restless lately, and she was strong-willed. She might do this just to spite him. It was something she would think to do, to taunt him, to make him know all the more how very much he loved her.

The letters looked uninteresting, and he tossed them aside. Then he noticed one with a Feather Island postmark. He tore it open. It was typewritten, and there was no signature.

"I know what you've done with Ilsa. A hundred thousand dollars will keep my mouth shut. Wait for my next letter and instructions."

XVII

THAT MORNING Eric Channon did not take the ferry as he usually did. Ruby had phoned him about the trouble at the South Wind. When he reached the hotel, he parked his car and looked at the damage. A small dog came barking at him, and Eric tried to shoo him away. Then Scott Stoner came to claim the mongrel.

"Sorry. Mops isn't usually hostile like this. Real mess, isn't it?" he asked, nodding to the patched window.

"No one ever breaks a *little* window," Eric said. "Alway the big one. I suppose it could have been worse."

Eric went inside. No one was at the desk. He made his way to the office door and knocked. Wynne was there. She was startled to see him.

"Ruby phoned," he said. "I'm sorry about your trouble."

"Will my insurance cover it?"

"Yes. I'll have the adjuster come and take a look, make an estimate."

Wynne was so lovely. Sometimes he forgot that. She came as a kind of shock. Had he grown so used to Karen's pixie, girlish ways?

"While I'm here, it would be a good time to discuss increasing your coverage."

"I'm sure we have enough," Wynne replied.

"Everything costs so much more than it did. If you suffered any large loss, you'd come out in the red. Let me leave you some figures, and you can discuss it with your grandmother."

Wynne's face went pale. Eric knew something was wrong. He knew Wynne too well. Had she quarreled with the old lady? Well, that was par for the course. She ought to have known it wasn't going to be easy. Harvey Russell had learned that.

He did a little quick figuring, put it all on a fresh sheet of paper for her and put it on the desk.

"Several thousand dollars more coverage won't be that expensive, Wynne. I advise you to take it. Better safe than sorry."

"You weren't at the party last night," Wynne said.

"No."

"Aren't you and Max Hethershaw on the same side of the fence?"

Eric blinked. "I hardly know Max Hethershaw!"

"But you want the bridge. Good for business, I suppose. Have you become such a commercialist, Eric?"

He felt the pulse pounding in his throat. She knew. Somehow, she knew about the committee and his part in it! He swallowed hard.

"If I have, you've put on blinders, Wynne. As sure as you're sitting there, the island is ripe for changes. You can't hold today still. You can't keep yesterday. There's always tomorrow."

"No, we can't keep yesterday," she replied, and there was steel in her voice.

Suddenly, the quarrel was not about the island at all. It was about them. Eric got slowly to his feet. He looked at her for a long moment. He went around the desk to her and took her hands in his.

"Wynne, forgive me. For everything. Can't you do that?"

"Does it matter?"

"Yes!" Eric said. "It matters very much."

She pulled her hands away. "I've never had the pleasure of meeting your fiancée."

Eric's throat went dry. "She's a nice girl."

"I'm sure of it. But tell her to beware. I just had a letter in the mail today. The Grants are due in at the end of the week. Perhaps Shelley will be with them."

Eric swallowed hard. He didn't know what to do or say. Wynne gave him a cool smile. Did she hate him now? Perhaps. He didn't know. He only knew that he wanted to leave before the room smothered him.

111

He snatched up his briefcase and moved to the door. "Give me a call about the insurance figures, will you, please?"

He darted out of the lobby, past the front desk, and on to his car. He drove recklessly down to the dock. Sam was sitting in the sun, cap over his eyes. He had to shake him to wake him up.

"Can you run me over, Sam?" Eric asked.

Sam stretched and got lazily to his feet. "I reckon I can. How come you missed the regular run this morning?"

"Business. With Wynne."

"I heard about it. I suppose she asked for it."

Eric was shocked. Captain Sam had always been one of Wynne's closest friends.

"You condone what's happened?"

Sam was testy. "Didn't say that. But she ought to know she was asking for trouble, putting up those four fellows."

"It's still a free country, Sam. Who pitched the rock? Do you have any idea?"

Sam frowned. "Do you think I'm fool enough to open my big mouth, even if I did?"

Eric knotted his fists. He felt a little sick to his stomach. "I feel sorry for Wynne. When her old friends betray her, what chance has the girl got?"

For a moment, Eric thought he was going to get Sam's fist in his mouth. Then, the old man stomped away to the ferry and motioned for him to drive aboard. The rest of the way across the sound to Charlton, Sam didn't speak to him again.

When Eric reached Charlton, he didn't go to his office. He went instead to find Delmer.

"Why, Eric, my boy. What brings you?" Delmer asked.

Eric sat down in front of Delmer's desk. "I want it straight, Delmer. Is the committee behind the trouble on the island?"

Delmer folded his arms. "No. I heard about the South Wind. Unfortunate. A small incident really. But significant. The longer this goes, the worse it's going to be. I've put pressure on a few people. They're going to hurry up the surveys. Perhaps move on the bridge quicker than we expected."

"Then it's cut and dried?"

Delmer shook his head. "No. Not really. But the possibility is growing stronger and stronger."

"Who's behind it, Delmer. If you know, for God's sake, tell me!" Eric said. "I live over there. I do business with those people! They're my friends. I don't like the look of any of this."

"A crackpot. Someone with a grudge."

"Someone who wants no part of the bridge or anyone connected with it, even in the most remote way! This is getting serious, Delmer!"

"There's been a petition. Backed by Priscilla Russell. She has influence in high places."

Eric licked his lips. "You mean she has a chance of stopping it?"

"I honestly don't know. But I hope not. We've worked too hard to get it. We can't lose it now."

"The island people can only sit and wait, is that it? The development people want the island. They've wanted it for a long time. It's useless without the bridge. Who has more power? A handful of people on the island? Priscilla Russell? Or some big shot in Tallahassee?"

Eric stopped. He was getting angry. Too angry.

Delmer gave him a thoughtful smile. "It doesn't ride easy does it, straddling the fence."

Eric cooled down and managed a laugh. "No. It doesn't ride a bit easy."

"Take my word for it, Eric. We threw no rocks last night. We all want the bridge, and we want it badly, but there's not a man on the committee that would stoop that low. It's a crackpot, Eric. Just a crackpot."

When Brad came down from his room after the party, he saw Eric Channon just leaving the hotel. Glancing in the office, he saw Wynne sitting at her desk, white-faced and angry. He decided not to call or stop in. Instead, he went to the Hurricane and ate his usual large breakfast. Johnny was waiting for him, and while Brad ate, he loaded the diving gear aboard the *Lazy Day*.

When Brad went aboard, he spent a few minutes with his charts. Johnny bent over for a look.

"This isn't Dolphin Bay!"

"No. We're going north. Up around Egret Bay."

Johnny blinked. "At Hethershaw's place?"

"That's right. They tell me that water is dangerous there. If you don't want to come along, Johnny—"

"Sure thing!" Johnny said. "What are we waiting for?"

In a few minutes, they had the boat revved up and the mooring lines tossed inside. Brad eased the boat away from the dock and started along the coast line toward Egret Bay. The sun was bright. But there were clouds on the horizon, and they would bear watching.

"Turn on the radio. Get the marine band, Johnny. Pick up the weather if you can."

But there were no warnings. Just the usual chatter, and as they neared Egret Bay, Brad cut the motor and let it drift. From here, he had a good view of the Hethershaw house. It looked like a doll house up on the high cliff. Down the coast was Priscilla Russell's house, nearly as attractive, but older, less flamboyant.

"Are you going to dive here, Brad?"

"For a starter," he said. "Then we'll work closer to the rocks."

"My sister works up there," Johnny said.

"I know." Brad grinned. "Where's she keeping herself?"

"She's staying up there all the time. Sort of funny about that."

Brad was checking his air tanks for a second time. "What do you mean, funny?"

"Lorrie's been as jumpy as a cat lately. Nervous, you know. I heard her crying one night. But she wouldn't tell me why."

Brad shrugged. "Girls are like that, Johnny."

"Not Lorrie. Nothing ever made her cry before. Not even when Pa—"

Johnny broke off. Brad knew Will Dykes on sight and on sight, did not like the man. A time or two, Johnny had hinted that he and his sister were mistreated by their father.

"Let's get busy, Johnny. I want to make one dive before those clouds get any closer. Could be some rain in them. Wind too."

In a few minutes, he was jumping overboard and going down into the green depths of the ocean. He saw nothing unusual. Seaweed, fish, coral. Then he felt three jerks on the line and knew that Johnny was signaling him to come up. He'd been down only a very few minutes. It had hardly been worthwhile. But Johnny had been trained, and he knew never to signal him unless it was important.

He started back up, and when he emerged near the boat, he saw at once what was wrong. The clouds were bearing down and coming fast. It looked like one of those tricky summer squalls that blew in along the coast from time to time.

Johnny helped heave him into the boat, and he got out of some of his gear.

"Start up, Johnny. We'll make a run for it?"

"We'll never get back to the dock! Not now. The rain's starting."

He had two choices. Hethershaw's place or the Russell dock. The rocks could be dangerous.

"The Russell beach!" he shouted to Johnny. "Let's go."

The water was quickly growing choppy. It took all of Brad's brains and skill to land them safely. They moored the boat and ran for the safety of the trees.

As quickly as it had come up, the storm blew itself out.

"OK. We can go back out now."

On their way back to the boat, Brad noticed something half buried in the sand. It was a woman's purse! He shook the sand off. It was white. Leather. Expensive. He had difficulty in opening the zipper. Inside, everything was soaked, but there was a wallet. A plastic window had kept the identification partially dry and readable.

"Ilsa Hethershaw!"

"Boy, there's money in the wallet," Johnny said. "What will we do with it?"

Brad put the wallet back inside and closed the zipper. "I'll take it up to the house later. Now come on, Johnny. The day's wasting."

XVIII

When Brad and Johnny put into shore that evening, Brad saw the old truck parked near the hotel and Lorrie waiting. She waved as he walked toward her. Johnny was busy making the boat fast and gathering up the gear to store in the hotel.

"Have a good day?" Lorrie asked.

"An interesting one. Listen, how about something cold to drink? I'm parched. The sun was very hot after the rain this morning."

He had the purse wrapped in an old jacket under his arm. Lorrie fell in step beside him. A very tiny young woman. Her head barely came to his shoulder.

"Aren't you staying up on the hill tonight?" Brad asked.

"No," Lorrie shook her head. "My work is finished there. With Ilsa away——"

Brad guided Lorrie into a corner booth at the Hurricane which was more secluded than some of the others. The supper crowd had not yet gathered. The place was quiet. Ruby brought them cold lemonade, and when she had gone, Brad unwrapped the purse.

"Do you recognize this?" he asked.

Lorrie gasped. "Why, it's Ilsa's!"

"Does she usually take such expensive bags sailing or anything?"

Lorrie's brown eyes were very wide and startled. "No. Of course not. Where did you find it?"

"We found it on the beach near the Russell house. There's identification in it, but I wanted to be sure. I'll return it tonight."

Lorrie grasped his arm. "First, Wynne finds a scarf. Now you've found the purse——"

"I think Ilsa Hethershaw must be a reckless young

116

woman with her belongings," Brad said. "Suppose I might collect a reward? If I do, I promised half to Johnny."

Lorrie seemed upset.

"Is something wrong?" Brad asked.

Lorrie shook her head quickly. "No. Of course not. But I wouldn't count on a reward from Max. You probably won't even get past Mattie. Max doesn't encourage visitors."

"After giving such a big party?" Brad said. "That doesn't make sense."

"The party was for Ilsa, the missing hostess."

"I didn't see you there," Brad said pointedly.

"I was helping Mattie. In the kitchen."

"Too bad. I looked for you. We could have had a dance or two."

Lorrie smiled. She was a very pretty girl. Her brown eyes gave him a quick, guarded look. There was something about the girl. A certain unhappiness. Like a bird caught in mid flight and not knowing whether to keep on soaring or fall to the earth.

"How about going for a long boat ride tonight? Maybe to Charlton. We could have dinner and that dance we missed last night."

She gave him a smile. "All right, Brad. That sounds like fun."

"I'll come over and pick you up at Sam's dock. Say about seven o'clock."

Later at the hotel, he borrowed Wynne's car and made his way up the hill to the Hethershaw house.

It was particularly impressive this time of day. The sun was hovering over the horizon, and the sea seemed calm. Perhaps it was even a little too calm. Could another storm be building up out there in the Gulf?

He brought the car to a halt and strode toward the door, the purse under his arm. He knocked loudly, and when no one answered, he knocked again.

At last, the door came open. The maid, a rather forbidding type of woman, stood there.

"I'd like to see Mr. Hethershaw," Brad said.

"He's not receiving visitors. Sorry."

She started to close the door in his face, but he was too agile for her. He stepped inside.

117

"I wanted to return this. I found it on the beach today," Brad said. "It was probably washed up at high tide."

He held up the white purse, and Mattie's solemn face seemed to flinch for a moment.

"I'll see that he gets it."

"I'd like to explain to Max where I found it," Brad said persistently.

"Sorry."

There was nothing he could do but go. Mattie wasted no time in slamming and locking the door behind him. Strange. What odd people! At the party, there couldn't have been a more social and personable man than Max Hethershaw. But today, he wasn't receiving guests! He'd heard about the islanders' reserve, but this was hard to believe.

Brad drove back down to the hotel and went straight to his room. Wynne wasn't at the desk or in the office when he came back down and walked to the dock and the *Lazy Day*. The water at night was different. He anticipated the ride to Charlton and back. It would be fun. Frankly, he'd rather have been taking Wynne out, but Lorrie was nice too.

He rounded the island, passing Dolphin Bay and Eric Channon's house. Then he buzzed along in the twilight toward the dock at Sam's place. He saw Lorrie waiting there wearing a yellow dress, her blond hair flying in the breeze. She saw him coming and waved.

He eased up to the dock and helped her aboard.

"Hey, you smell real nice and look good enough to eat."

She smiled. "Did you return the purse?"

"Yes. And you were right. I couldn't get past Mattie."

Lorrie frowned. "I wonder what Max must have thought—"

"Let's forget the Hethershaws," Brad said. "I did my good deed of the day, so now, let's concentrate on having a good time."

He talked about North Dakota as they crossed the sound to Charlton. Lorrie seemed interested in what he did and where he lived. She seemed pathetically intrigued by anything or anyplace away from Feather Island.

"You feel trapped, don't you, Lorrie?"

"Yes."

"Pardon my saying so, but Johnny hinted a time or two that things aren't exactly rosy for you at home."

"Johnny should learn to keep his mouth shut!" she said quickly.

"I think he needed to talk about it. To someone like me. Believe me, I'll keep everything he said confidential."

"I'm sorry. I want you to know that I appreciate all you've done for Johnny. He's crazy about this boat and going out with you. You've been good for him."

"I sort of like him too," Brad said with a grin. "I'm used to kids. I can usually sort out the good apples from the rotten ones. Johnny's got the making of something pretty special, I think. He's a little green right now, but he'll ripen."

When they reached Charlton, Brad called a cab. Lorrie suggested a nice place where they might go for dinner.

It was a quiet supper club. A little on the glamorous side, but he knew Lorrie was loving every minute. He bought her lobster and watched her enjoy it. The little line that sometimes creased her brow had finally disappeared. She seemed relaxed. Almost happy.

They danced to several numbers. She seemed very tiny in his arms. It would be no effort at all to pick her up and toss her in the air like some little child. Returning to the table, he saw her cheeks were flushed and her eyes bright.

"Lorrie, you're Wynne's best friend, aren't you?"

"Yes."

"What about Eric Channon?"

"You know about him?"

"Not much. But I'm curious."

"Once they were in love. Then there was trouble. They broke up."

"How does Wynne feel about that now?"

"I'm not sure. Why do you ask?"

"Wynne's a great girl. A real great girl."

Lorrie blinked and lowered her head. "Yes, she is."

She suddenly grew very quiet. After a short time, Brad suggested they go. It seemed she was no longer enjoying the evening. She was almost remote. Even as they skimmed the water of the sound heading for the light on Sam's dock, she was withdrawn. What had he done? Girls! They were never easy to understand.

At the dock, he wanted to walk her home, but she leaped out agilely and shook her head.

"You don't need to do that. It's just a few steps. Goodnight, Brad. Thanks for a nice evening."

"Sure. It was fun, wasn't it. See you around. Goodnight, Lorrie."

Then Lorrie disappeared. In the starlight, he caught a glimpse of her yellow dress, like a moth suddenly disappearing into the dark.

Before Lorrie left to keep her date with Brad, Will Dykes had overheard her talking with Johnny about finding the purse. All Johnny could think about was getting a reward. Will scoffed to himself. Johnny had a lot to learn in this world! People like Max Hethershaw didn't go around doing anyone a favor. Not unless someone was putting the heat on or twisting his arm a little. Max liked it that way. Sittin' up there in his fancy house making like a lord or something.

Funny though, Brad and Johnny finding that purse. Real strange. Maybe rich people threw away expensive things for a kick. Or were so careless with their belongings, they didn't care if they were lost. Still—Will rubbed his whiskery face. There was something he was missing here. It nagged at him. He'd heard about Ilsa not being at the party. He'd had an invitation, but he hadn't bothered with it. He'd rather stay home at night on the front steps and watch the lights of Charlton across the sound.

Ilsa had been called away. Family emergency, Max had said. Only Ilsa didn't have any family. She'd told him so herself once. Just a stepbrother somewhere. Chicago, if he remembered right. Somehow, he didn't think Ilsa had left a glamorous party to go to the bedside of a stepbrother. Ilsa wasn't the type. She'd rather sashay around in some pretty dress and flirt with the men.

But she hadn't been there. Folks were wondering about it too. Did she really have an emergency or had she just decided she didn't want to mix with the island people?

Who could tell? Ilsa thought she was somebody all right.

Will went to sit on the front step for a while. He kept thinking about Max Hethershaw and what he'd told him about Ilsa. Maybe there was a connection between that and Ilsa not being at the party.

After a while, he ambled down to Sam's place. He'd seen Sam make a ferry run to Charlton, but he was back now, lounging in the old chair out in front of his office.

"Warm night," Will said.

"Getting ready for another squall, I suppose," Sam said.

"Could I bother you for my mail? I'm expecting some parts I ordered."

Sam grumbled and finally unlocked the post office and gave him three packages. One of them was exactly what he wanted.

"Got Ilsa's repairs here," Will said. "But I reckon she took the car when she left the island. I suppose I'll get left holding the sack for the cost of this."

"Ilsa didn't go in her car," Sam said. "Unless it sprouted fins and swam over by itself."

"That right?" Will said.

"Didn't take her. She must have went by boat."

"Yeah, I reckon. Well, maybe tomorrow I'll go up that way and see about putting this in. 'Night, Sam."

Will figured he'd go up to Hethershaw's tomorrow when he got around to it. He wanted his money for this part. He wanted pay for his trouble. Fact was, he sort of liked being around Hethershaw, just to see him sweat a little. It was something new for Will Dykes to have power over the big man. But he did. He knew something about Ilsa. He'd seen her that day with a man. Just a glimpse, but enough. Enough to make Hethershaw anxious to stay on the good side of him.

The next morning, Will ate his breakfast in silence. Lorrie was underfoot again. Itching to get out. But Will didn't figure she was going anywhere. Not until he said so. Johnny was off and gone at sunrise. Crazy about that Brad Sherman and the boat and all that diving.

All in all, it was the middle of the morning before

121

Will drove up the winding hill to the Hethershaw house. He went to the back door and demanded to see Max.

Mattie was not one of his greatest admirers. She told him Hethershaw was busy.

"Well, tell him I have to see him. I've got Ilsa's car repair here. Want to put it in."

"Car's not here. Now, go away and don't bother us," Mattie said crossly.

Mattie shut the door in his face. Will swore bitterly. Then taking the package under his arm, he stomped back to the truck. On second thought, he went to look in the garage. Mattie was right. Ilsa's little red automobile wasn't there. But last night, Sam said he'd never taken Ilsa on the ferry. How else could Ilsa get the car off the island?

"Downright peculiar," Will muttered to himself. "Where the hell is the car anyway?"

XIX

WYNNE THOUGHT each day she would hear from Grandmother. But there was no word. No phone call. No summons to come to the house. Just an icy silence. It wore Wynne's nerves raw. She had enough trouble on her hands without adding Grandmother's anger to it. The coolness of the islanders at Max Hethershaw's party had cut deeply. They were old friends! Now, they had all turned against her. All because she had dared to rent rooms to four men who were surveying for the bridge!

Scott knew how upset she was. He did his best to cheer her and invited her to dinner at the Hurricane.

"I might not be the best of company," she warned.

"You'd always be great company," he said warmly. Then a little frown creased his forehead. "I have something important to tell you."

"You make it sound mysterious."

"Not mysterious. Just about me. And what I'm doing."

Her brows went up at that. With a laugh, he blew her a kiss and hurried away up the steps. "I'll knock on your apartment door at seven."

When he came, Mops was at his heels. While they went inside the Hurricane, Mops waited at the door.

They enjoyed one of Ruby's good meals, and Wynne waited impatiently for Scott to explain, to tell her what he'd promised to tell.

"Wynne, would you take a drive with me? I think it might be the simplest way to explain things. I've sent in my reports, and I've finished my work here."

They left the Hurricane, and Mops leaped into the car with them. Scott drove away from the hotel and took the road south. Just before he reached Dolphin Bay, he turned off to a little used road. There was nothing much here but mangrove trees and sand. He stopped the car and got out.

"Come this way, Wynne."

She couldn't imagine what he had found here that he wanted to show her. This part of the island was the least inhabited. Then, she saw the stakes. Several of them.

"You're a surveyor!"

"I'm an engineer. I've been making soil borings, looking for the best spot on the island. This was it. I was asked to stake it out."

A building this size could only be—a hotel!

"I see," she said weakly. "I understand."

"I wanted you to know. I wanted you to be forewarned. Most of this has been done on the q.t. I shouldn't have told you. But I couldn't let you hear about it from someone else."

"A big fancy hotel?"

"Very big. Very fancy. Catering to every tourist whim you can think of."

"Who will be the owners?"

"I'm sorry. I can't tell you that, as much as I would like to."

"Does anyone on the island know about this?"

"I've tried to be discreet. If anyone knows, I haven't been approached about it."

"They've been too busy breaking out my windows!" she said bitterly.

"I've felt like a traitor, working here," he said. "But I was hired, I've been paid. I had to complete the work."

Wynne looked about. Here nature still grew wild.

Birds nested in the trees. It was almost a sanctuary for many wild things. But if the bulldozers came, the cement truckers, the carpenters, the masons, the wild things would be either killed or frightened away and deprived of their natural homes. It sickened her to think about it.

"Oh, Scott, I hate to see it come."

He put his arms around her. His lips brushed her forehead.

"I know. I understand. Man seems set on spoiling everything he touches. The next thing you know, you'll

124

be having sewage problems, fouled water, fouled air, and something will be gone forever. But how do we stop it?"

Mops had been let out to run, and he was having a grand time darting in and around the trees, startling the birds, and being very noisy and frolicsome. Scott whistled for him.

"Come on, Mops. Time to go."

Then suddenly, they heard a howl of pain. Something had happened to the dog. Scott ran, and Wynne followed.

It took a few seconds to find him. Somehow, he had become pinned under a large rock. Mops was howling, struggling to be free.

"He must have jumped across these when I whistled, lost his balance, and dislodged one of the stones as he fell!"

Scott was only a moment in freeing the little dog. The dog wailed in pain, and Scott lifted him into his arms.

"It's his leg. Broken perhaps. We'll have to get him to a vet, Wynne."

"There's a good one in Charlton. Doctor Jameson."

"Will you drive?"

Scott held the dog tenderly, stroking his head, and talking to him to comfort him. Wynne drove straight to Sam's ferry. Sam looked at Wynne from beneath the brim of his cap, but she couldn't determine his expression.

"What happened?" he asked.

"An accident," Scott replied. "I think he's got a broken leg. Would you take us across? We've got to find a vet."

Sam hesitated.

"Please, Sam," Wynne said.

He muttered something to himself, and after a moment, motioned them to drive aboard. When they were under way, Wynne went to join Sam at the wheel. He barely acknowledged her presence, but kept his eyes on the lights of Charlton.

"Still angry with me?" she asked.

He didn't reply. She put her hand over his on the wheel.

"Don't be, Sam. Please. If you're against me, how can I bear it? What was I to do? Turn them away? They're decent men. Doing their job. For that matter, you

125

brought them over, didn't you? But no one sabotaged you, did they?"

Sam cleared his throat. "Nope. I reckon you got a point. I reckon we're all so stirred up, none of us is thinking straight. I've been wrong. I'm sorry, girl."

She laughed with relief. With a quick hug, she kissed his weathered cheek.

"Sam, I love you! I knew you wouldn't let me down when I needed you."

"Everybody's going crazy," Sam said. "Me included. Maybe when things are settled for once and for all, we'll come to our senses."

She leaned her head against his shoulder for a moment, remembering the stakes that Scott had set and what would probably take root there.

A new hotel would drive her right out of business. The South Wind couldn't compete. It was too old, too shabby, too small. Oh, but she loved every inch of it! She loved the way it hugged the beach, a little weathered but solid. She loved the way the afternoon sun flooded the lobby, the familiar homey atmosphere with its faded carpeting, its old but comfortable furniture. It was home. Not only to her. But to many others. Home to George Laughlin. A summer home, but a very special one, to the Wilkin twins. And there were many others who came regularly in the wintertime and felt warmly toward it.

"I'm sorry about your window, Wynne. It was a mean thing to do," Sam said.

"I wonder, Sam, will we survive all of this?"

But Sam had no answer. If the bridge came, Sam would be out of work. There would be no need for the ferry. What would he do? Perhaps the post office would be enough. If the island grew, so would the post office. But still, it was an ache in the heart to think *The Lady* would make no more runs.

When they reached Charlton, they asked Sam to wait, and within another fifteen minutes, Mops was on the vet's examination table.

"Is his leg broken?" Scott asked anxiously.

"No. Badly sprained. Not broken. But I think a splint

126

will be in order. He'll be able to hobble around in a day or two."

Scott laughed with relief. He ruffled the dog's fur.

"Good boy. I'm glad to hear it."

The vet gave the dog a shot and fixed the leg. Mops was still very sleepy when they carried him back to the car.

"Want to hold him?" Scott asked with a grin.

Wynne nodded.

He nestled in Wynne's lap and looked at her with his sleepy brown eyes. He seemed to enjoy all the attention that he was getting.

Sam was still waiting. They got under way and rode across the dark water under the stars. Mops had fallen asleep in the car. Wynne and Scott stood at the railing. Scott put his arm around her shoulder, and she leaned against him. He seemed so solid. So comfortable.

"Darling, I must tell you something else," Scott said. "Something I've wanted to say for a long time now— Almost since the first day I saw you at the hotel."

She turned in his arms and touched his lean face. He kissed the tips of her fingers.

"Wynne, I love you."

She lowered her head. The words shot through her. Then Scott lifted her chin, and his lips claimed hers, warmly, eagerly, passionately.

"You're everything I ever wanted, Wynne. Everything I've dreamed of finding. I want to put down roots. I want to put them down with you. I want a home. Kids. A real life."

She covered his lips with her fingers. "Please, don't say any more. Not just yet."

"Whatever happens, Wynne, remember that I love you. I will always love you."

XX

Max would not leave the house. He felt like a caged animal. He spent the days pacing up and down, leaping to answer the phone whenever it rang, pawing through the mail like a madman.

First the scarf. Then the note. The diver Brad Sherman returning Ilsa's purse. It was all building up inside with a tremendous pressure. Where was it all going to end? He couldn't eat, and he barely slept. Mattie began to watch him closely.

"Mr. Hethershaw, what's troubling you?" she asked.

"Business matter. A very pressing business matter. Mattie, take the car. Go down and get the evening mail. It should be there by now."

Mattie disliked driving. But she didn't argue. He paced about ceaselessly, waiting for her to return. It seemed she was gone hours. The hands on his watch barely moved. At last, he heard her coming and went to the door to meet her.

He thumbed through the mail frantically. Nothing. Just a few business letters from Charlton. It meant waiting until tomorrow's mail. Waiting and waiting and waiting!

Oh, Ilsa, he thought. Ilsa!

The night was intolerably long. Exhaustion gave him a few hours' sleep. But he woke up with a start, wringing wet, heart pounding.

The next morning, he could not bear to wait for Mattie to drive down to the post office, so he went himself, driving very fast. When he reached the dock, the ferry was not there, and the post office was locked. He was too early. He smoked one cigarette after another, walking up and down the dock, footsteps echoing hollowly over the water. Then at last, he saw *The Lady* coming. Very slowly. Sam never knew how to hurry.

When Sam finally unlocked the post office, Max stepped in. He saw the letter in his box at once and plucked it out. The typing was the same. The same kind of white envelope.

"Sam, when did you put this in my box?"

"Last night. Late. Someone mailed it after the post office closed. Hey, where you going. Don't you want the morning mail?" Sam shouted after him. "The *Wall Street Journal?*"

He rushed out to his car and drove away. The letter lay on the seat beside him, and when he had gotten far enough down the road that Sam couldn't see him, he stopped and ripped it open. The message was terse and to the point.

"You have twenty-four hours to get $100,000 in small unmarked bills. Instructions follow. P.S. Have you visited Sunset Point lately?"

Max wadded the letter with a muttered oath. He drove like a man possessed, his car zooming along the twisting roads at a reckless speed. As he passed the South Wind Hotel, he saw George Laughlin look after him curiously. He must be careful. He must not attract attention. He must not make anyone suspicious. But somehow, he couldn't make himself drive more slowly.

Reaching the house, he put the car in the garage. Then with swift steps, he walked toward Sunset Point, following a path from the house.

Sunset Point was one of the finest places on the island. It looked out to the sea from a dizzy height. Immediately below were the treacherous waters of Egret Bay. They were especially dangerous and deep just below Sunset Point. He reached the point and paused. It took him only a moment to see the tracks in the sand. Car tracks. With a gasp, he saw that they went to the very edge of the point. A car had gone over! It must have gone out of control and smashed into the rocks and sunk in the water below!

His throat went dry. The tracks were narrow. The treads deep. Much like the kind of tires on Ilsa's car— his head was in a whirl. His stomach pitched. He took

129

one more look at the water below. It was impossible! Totally impossible!

He rushed back to the house, his gray hair ruffled, his composure destroyed.

"Mornin', Max," Will Dykes said.

Max came to a halt. He hadn't seen Will standing there with a grin on his face, a toothpick in his mouth.

"What is it you want, Will?"

Will held up a small package. "I've got Ilsa's car repairs here. Cost me a pretty penny. I want my money. Stopped yesterday. Didn't Mattie tell you?"

"How much is it?"

Will gave him a figure. Max fumbled in his wallet and pressed the money in his hand along with a sizable tip. Will laughed.

"Now, that's right generous of you, Max. Especially considering there ain't no car for me to repair."

Max swallowed hard. "You can put on the new parts when Ilsa comes back."

Max turned away, but Will called to him again. "Now, Max, you and me both know that might be a little hard."

Max stared at Will. "What do you mean?"

Will shifted his stance, scuffling his worn boots in the sand.

"Sam tells me he didn't take Ilsa and the little red car off the island. But it ain't in the garage. Know something else? I got a hunch it ain't on the island anywhere. I reckon you've seen those tracks over there at Sunset Point, same as me."

Max saw red. He lost all reason. Never before in all of his life had he struck a man a blow with his fists. But he did now. To his surprise, he found Will lying on his back at his feet.

"That won't do you any good, Max," Will said.

"So, it's you! You're sending the letters—"

Will blinked. "I don't know anything about any letters. I just got an idea that little red car—"

Max knew instantly that the letters couldn't be from Will. Will wouldn't be smart enough to figure out anything like that. Will was more direct. Oh he liked to see a man suffer. He took pure delight in it. But he couldn't be the blackmailer.

130

Max jerked Will to his feet. "Sorry, Will. Lost my temper. I've—I've been worried about Ilsa. She got angry with me. In spite, she sent the car over the cliff at Sunset Point. Then she left me. Will, I want you to do something for me."

Will folded his arms over his faded shirt and laughed.

"Sure, Max. Sure. What you want me to do?"

"Don't tell anyone about this. I mean—well, it's embarrassing. Understand?"

Will gloated. Max began pouring it on. He filled Will's ears with all sorts of nonsense, but Will swallowed it all. To seal the whole business, Max reached into his wallet again and found a couple of bills. He tucked them into Will's shirt pocket.

"Our secret, Will? I'd surely appreciate it."

Will laughed in an ugly way. "You think you can buy something like that for a couple of twenty-dollar bills? Not hardly, Mr. Hethershaw."

Max was perspiring. His hands were cold. His brain was running in a dozen directions at once.

"What is it you want?"

"When the bridge comes, I'll be needing a nice new place of business. Always wanted a gas station. Six pumps. Real shiny and fancy. But that takes money."

Max took a deep breath. "I'll see you get a good loan, Will. I'll help you in any way I can, with right-of-way or whatever—"

Will nodded. "All right, Max. Always knew you were a gentleman. A real fine gentleman."

Then Will tipped his grease-stained cap and walked away. Max went into the house. He closed and locked the door behind him. Then he went straight out to the balcony and looked to the bay toward Sunset Point.

Ilsa's car was down there. Almost certainly. And someone knew it. Someone thought he'd done it. Was Ilsa down there too?

He felt ill again. Truly ill. He had been up against all kinds of odds in his day. He'd dealt with all kinds of people. He was not a poker player. But he recognized a stacked deck when he saw it. Someone would see the blame was put on him unless he paid the hundred thousand dollars.

Getting his binoculars, he looked down to the point, looking for God knew what. Anything that looked like a little red car. But there was nothing visible. Nothing caught on the rocks or strewn along the face of the cliff. If it was there, it was under the water.

Then as he raised the glasses, he saw the *Lazy Day*. Johnny Dykes and that diver Brad Sherman! They were coming into the bay. Were they heading for Sunset Point?

XXI

THE WILKIN TWINS were complaining again about Diane Carlson and her noisy typewriter. Wynne listened patiently while Nettie raved on. Lettie stood to one side, plainly embarrassed.

"I'll speak with Miss Carlson," Wynne said at last. "Perhaps we can arrange for her to move to another room. I'll do something."

"I should hope so!" Nettie said with a sniff.

With that, the twins marched away, and Wynne took a deep breath. It was just a minor thing. But it went with the hotel business.

She was just ready to knock on Miss Carlson's door when Marge came out of Edward Allen's room at the end of the hall.

"Wynne, could you come here a minute?"

She followed Marge into Edward's room. "The faucet is leaking a stream. I wonder why he hasn't reported it," Marge said.

"Edward strikes me as being the type who doesn't want to be a bother. I'll tell Pete about it. Probably he can fix it."

"I don't know. These faucets are getting awfully old."

Wynne nodded. How true! Everything about the hotel was beginning to show its age. She glanced around the room. Edward lived like a Spartan. There were few personal belongings visible. Just a hair brush on the chest and a small portable typewriter opened on a night stand. It was a foreign make, a machine Wynne was not familiar with.

"You know something," Marge said with a frown. "Edward has put a lock on the closet. A new lock."

"Well, bless him!" Wynne laughed.

"What's he hiding?"

"Probably just a distrustful soul by nature. Hotels do get robbed sometimes, and perhaps he's had just such an experience."

"What's he got in there?"

"I wish it were Fort Knox and he'd give us a loan, Marge," Wynne laughed. "I'll find Pete as soon as I've talked to Miss Carlson."

Her visit with Diane Carlson took but a few minutes. She accepted the idea of moving with a quick nod of her head.

"As a matter of fact, those two old ladies over there don't give *me* any peace. They're always knocking on the wall or shouting at me to be quiet. How can I work in that kind of atmosphere?"

Wynne arranged with Marge to move Miss Carlson and was glad that at least this one small problem was solved. Last night, she had broken a house rule and allowed Scott to bring Mops up to his room. They'd made him a comfortable bed in an old cardboard box.

This morning, Scott had taken Mops with him and driven away in his car. Although he said his work was finished, he hadn't said anything about leaving.

Somehow, the thought of Scott being gone made her feel a little hollow inside. She remembered standing at the railing last night, she remembered his warm lips, the things he'd said. For a little while, she had found herself responding. She wanted to love Scott. She wanted to be head over heels in love with him! If only she could get Eric completely out of her heart.

It was the middle of the morning when Lorrie dropped by. She had walked from the house, and she looked hot and tired. Wynne sent her to the kitchen for something cold to drink.

"Wynne, have you talked to Brad?"

"No."

"Then you don't know about Ilsa's purse?"

Lorrie told her the entire story. "I knew something was going to happen," she added.

"Is this what's been bothering you? Lorrie, do you know more than you're telling me?"

"Ilsa had me deliver notes to Twin Palms. There was a certain hiding place."

"Another man?"

"I can only assume that. Why else would Ilsa be so secretive about it? But I have no idea who. Not the faintest notion. I didn't want to get involved. I didn't want to take any part in the charade."

"Then why—"

Lorrie brushed back a lock of hair and shook her head. "I had to," she said in a trembling voice. "I was forced. You don't know about Johnny. No one knows. Except Ilsa. He got into trouble."

Wynne blinked with surprise as Lorrie rushed on to explain.

"Some boys from Charlton came over, and they got the bright idea they'd take Ilsa's car out for a joy ride. They did. One night. Ilsa caught them red-handed. The others got away without being recognized. Johnny begged her not to tell Dad. You could imagine what that would be like."

Wynne nodded. "Yes."

"So Ilsa told me. She's been holding it over my head ever since."

"So, in return, you did favors. A kind of blackmail!"

"If Dad ever found out about Johnny—"

They were quiet for a few moments, contemplating that, and it was not a pretty picture.

"I'm only glad that Johnny is working these days," Lorrie said. "By the way, I went to Charlton last night with Brad. For dinner."

There was a flush to Lorrie's cheeks. A brightness in her eyes. Was Brad responsible for this?

"Did you have a nice time?"

"Yes. Very nice. Did you realize Brad is very fond of you? Perhaps more than just fond?"

Wynne laughed. "Brad's a friend. Nothing more."

Lorrie gave her a quick look. "No. It's more than that, I'm sure."

"Then it's news to me," Wynne said.

"Will Brad and Johnny come ashore for lunch?"

"Sometimes they do. Why don't you wait and see. We'll all have lunch together."

Brad eased the *Lazy Day* toward Egret Bay. Then cutting the motor, he let them drift for a little while. It was a lovely place, but there was a kind of ruggedness about it that was peculiar to this end of the island. To the right of the Hethershaw house, there was a clearing that Johnny told him was Sunset Point.

"That's where I'd like to dive," Brad said, pointing. "Right up there between those rocks."

"That could be dangerous," Johnny said.

"You scared?"

"You're the one going down," Johnny said with a grin. "Unless you've changed your mind and will let me make a dive here."

"Not on your life," Brad shook his head. "I'd have to answer to your sister if I let you do a fool thing like that. Help me with the gear. I'll make a dive here first, and then this afternoon, we'll move in closer."

Brad was just halfway into his diving gear when suddenly something whistled past his head. It splashed in the water. Johnny looked up with a frown.

"What was that?"

"I don't know," Brad said. "Did you check those air tanks?"

"They're OK."

Once again there was a strange whistling sound. Then something thudded into the stern side of the boat.

"Hey!" Johnny said. "Brad, that was—"

Brad wasted no time. He leaped for the starter and prayed the engine would fire. Then with a roar and a quick turn of the wheel, they sped away.

"They were shooting at us, Brad! Somebody was shooting at us!"

Brad knew perfectly well what someone had been doing without Johnny shouting it in his ear. He didn't let up on his throttle until they were some distance from Egret Bay and the landing dock at the South Wind was in view.

"I don't think they were taking very good aim. On purpose," Brad said thoughtfully. "But they wanted to scare us out of there."

"Boy! They sure did that!" Johnny said, his brown eyes wide.

Brad reached out to grip Johnny's shoulder. "Johnny, you're not to mention this to anyone. Do you understand? No one. Unless I say so."

"But Brad—"

"No one," Brad said firmly. "Promise me."

"OK." Johnny said. "OK."

Brad knew the boy was excited about this. He naturally wanted to tell his friends. But not yet. Not until he could figure out just *why* someone was so determined to keep them away from Egret Bay.

As they pulled into the dock, Brad saw Lorrie waiting for them.

"What do you want, Sis?" Johnny asked.

Lorrie made a face at him. "I wanted to have lunch with you, do you mind?"

"Ah, crimney—"

Brad laughed. "That's no way to talk to a pretty lady, Johnny. Where's the other pretty one? Can't Wynne join us?"

"Edward's out. She's minding the desk. Actually, I did have another reason for coming, Brad," Lorrie said. "Would you like to come to supper tonight?"

"Yeah! That's a great idea," Johnny said. "You ought to taste her chocolate cake."

"I'm sorry," Brad shook his head. "I can't come tonight."

Lorrie's smile faded. "Perhaps another time," she murmured.

Brad had decided he was going back to Egret Bay. Tonight. After dark. He had made dives at night before, he could again. But he didn't want to risk taking Johnny with him. Who else was there that he could trust?

When they finished lunch, he told Johnny he intended to swim and relax in the sun. The boy seemed disappointed, and Brad knew he wanted to go back to Egret Bay too. But Brad couldn't risk taking him.

When Lorrie and Johnny had gone, Brad went to the South Wind and saw that Edward had returned. Wynne wasn't in the office.

"Where's Miss Russell?" Brad asked.

Edward gave him an owlish stare. "In her apartment probably. I don't know."

Brad stamped through the office and knocked at the adjoining door. In a moment, Wynne opened it.

"I'd like to speak with you," Brad said.

He closed the door carefully behind him. Wynne was fixing a snack in her small kitchen.

"Wynne, I want you to go out with me in the boat tonight. I need someone topside that I can trust. It's too risky to take Johnny. I want to go back to Egret Bay."

"At night? That place? What on earth for?"

"Someone seems to want me to stay away. I want to know why. Someone took some shots at Johnny and me this afternoon. Now, will you come?"

XXII

SUNSET MADE the water as red as blood. Wynne had begged Brad not to make this crazy trip. But he would not listen, and she could not let him go alone. So she found herself aboard the *Lazy Day*. They cruised around in the Gulf until it was dark. Then very carefully, they eased their way up along the coast toward Sunset Point.

"I think the shots came from up there, but I can't be sure," Brad said.

"Max Hethershaw?" Wynne asked.

"Possibly. Still, he doesn't strike me as the kind of man who would own a high-powered rifle."

Brad idled the motor, and for a few minutes, they rocked quietly on the waves. Brad took a pair of glasses and looked along the coast.

"Nothing. But it's hard to see anything at night. I'll get ready. The quicker I go down, the quicker I can come up. I'm going to ease up closer to the rocks and anchor there."

The night was deceptively calm. A few stars were shining, but there was a kind of heaviness in the air. A storm was brewing. Wynne knew the feeling. It was the very same way before a hurricane.

Brad got the boat into position and cut the motor. They waited for several minutes. Nothing happened.

"We're safe. I don't think anyone has spotted us," Brad said. "I'll make my dive as fast as I can. Keep your eye on the shore and the cliff, in particular. If you see anything at all, give three tugs on the rope. I'll come back up."

Then she watched Brad maneuver over the side of the boat, a waterproof lantern in his hand.

She shivered, although she was not cold. Once, she

139

thought she saw a light flash up at Sunset Point and then as quickly, go off. But she couldn't be sure. It was nerves. Just nerves. She wished she knew what time it was. How long had Brad been gone? It seemed hours. Surely it was only minutes.

She stared at the shore so hard, her eyes ached. Then suddenly, she felt Brad's signal. He was coming up! He couldn't get back too soon for her.

When he splashed overboard at last, she helped him with his gear.

"Start the motor, Wynne. Let's get out of here, fast!"

"Brad, what did you find?"

Brad gripped her hand for a moment. "A car. Ilsa Hethershaw's car!"

Wynne gasped. "You mean—Ilsa—"

"Just the car. Not Ilsa. It's possible she wasn't in the car when it went over. It's possible she was and was thrown out or has washed out since or—"

The horror of it gripped Wynne's throat like a tight hand. With numb fingers, she started the motor, and then Brad was there to handle the wheel. They eased away from Egret Bay as quietly as they could. Then when they were a safe distance away, Brad gave the motor full throttle. They couldn't talk above the roar. When they saw the lights on the dock at the hotel, Wynne knew they were both relieved.

A few minutes later, they were sitting in a booth at the Hurricane.

"What do we do about it, Brad?"

"I don't know. I suppose I must do something. Tell the police or Max or—"

"It all adds up," Wynne said. "The scarf. The purse. Now the car. Lorrie was right. She was so afraid there was something really wrong."

"How did you happen to find the scarf?" Brad asked. "What were you doing at Twin Palms?"

"That's the strange part. A note was left at the hotel. Typewritten. Supposedly from Lorrie asking me to meet her there. But Lorrie didn't write the note. In fact, she knew nothing about it."

Brad frowned. "Perhaps someone *wanted* you to find

140

the scarf. And perhaps this afternoon, the shots were fired only to rouse my natural curiosity. Maybe someone wanted me to go back there tonight and find the car!"

"And the purse was on the beach where anyone could have found it!" Wynne said. "But why?"

Brad shook his head. He leaned back in the booth, and he sipped his coffee. "I don't know. I think we'll sit on this for tonight anyway."

"Wynne—"

She looked around to see Scott. She smiled a welcome. Scott paused beside the booth.

"I'm sorry to interrupt, Wynne, but it's important. Could I speak with you?"

Brad got to his feet. "It's OK. I'm going back to the hotel anyway. I'll see you tomorrow, Wynne."

Scott took Brad's place. He put his hands on the table and met her eyes.

"Wynne, I'm not sure I know how to tell you this."

She studied his face. His hazel eyes were compassionate. He rumpled his hair and reached out to take her hand in his.

"Darling, I've had word. It came straight. Your grandmother's petition didn't do the job. It seems there was someone else with more influence in Tallahassee."

"Max Hethershaw?" Wynne asked.

"Perhaps. Probably. The thing is, the bridge is a fact now. Work will begin immediately. There's no longer any question about it."

Wynne lowered her head. She felt as if someone had given her a blow that snatched the air out of her lungs and left her dizzy, seeing strange lights and breathing much too fast.

"I'm sorry," Scott said. "I just wanted you to be prepared. Official word will be out tomorrow."

Wynne clung to Scott's hand for a moment. He tugged her to her feet and together, they walked out of the Hurricane and toward the South Wind. Scott led her out to the beach. The night seemed suddenly very oppressive. The air seemed heavier. The stars had gone.

"It's very close tonight," Scott said. "Does this mean a storm?"

141

"Perhaps."

"And tomorrow, there will be another kind of storm." Scott said. "How will your grandmother take it?"

She shook her head, and in a moment, she found herself in Scott's arms as she wept against his shoulder. He stroked her hair and rubbed away her tears.

"Don't, darling. Don't. You can't help this. No one can. You have to accept it."

"I'm not crying for myself," she said. "I'm crying for Grandmother."

"I know that, Wynne."

"I must go and tell her, Scott. It will be better coming from me than in a phone call or a letter—"

"Yes. Shall I drive you?"

"No. I'd better go alone."

Scott held her for a moment longer, and his kiss was tender, loving. He kept his arm around her as they walked back to the South Wind. Never had it looked so beguilingly beautiful, softened by the night, cradled in the arms of the tropic breeze.

Scott saw her to her car. In a few minutes, she was on the main road and driving slowly, dreading the encounter. She had not been here since they had quarreled about the survey crew. Now, she must break this awful news to her.

Wynne reached the house and walked up to the door. She lifted the knocker and let it fall. It took a few moments for Wilma to come to the door.

"I know it's late. But I must see Grandmother."

"She never goes to bed early, you know that," Wilma said. "I'm glad you've come. She has been—well—depressed since the other day—"

Wynne took her courage in hand. She was tempted to turn and run away. But there was no running away from this. There was no point in putting it off. The sooner Grandmother knew, the better.

Grandmother was reading, her cane hooked over the arm of her chair. The light from the reading lamp picked up the silvery whiteness of her hair.

"Grandmother—"

The book was lowered. Grandmother stared at her, her regal head lifting.

"It's very late," she said.

"I know," Wynne nodded. "But I had to come. I couldn't let this wait until morning. I thought you'd want to know—"

The words suddenly wouldn't come out. Wynne took the few steps across the room to the old lady and knelt down beside her. She took her hands tightly in her own.

"Grandmother, we've had our quarrels in the past. I know you're angry with me now. But that doesn't matter now. I've had it from a very reliable source that the—"

Grandmother flinched. "The bridge?"

"Yes. It's going to come. We've failed."

Grandmother sat very still, almost rigid. But her hands seemed suddenly cold, and her chin trembled. Her eyes were too bright, but she shed no tears. Then, she dropped her head, and she seemed very tired. She patted Wynne's shoulder. "Thank you for coming. Please go now. I'm very tired, and it's past my bedtime."

"Grandmother—"

She got to her feet. How small she was. How terribly tiny in this big, harsh world! Wynne's heart went out to her. She wanted to take her arm, to help her, but Grandmother shook her away.

"I'm all right. Good night, Wynne."

Then, she walked out of the room, cane tapping over the floor. In a distant part of the house, a door closed. The silence seemed very heavy. Overwhelming. Wynne rushed away to the door and out into the night, suddenly needing to run.

XXIII

Scott could not bring himself to go up to his room until Wynne had returned from her grandmother's house. He fully realized what a blow this was going to be to the old lady. Wynne felt deeply about it herself, but it would be doubly hard to tell her grandmother.

With Mops hobbling along beside him on his splinted leg, Scott paced about on the beach in front of the hotel.

This was such a peaceful spot. In a way, it made him think of Wyoming. There was the same open feeling here. Expanse. A remoteness. And for him, there was the same loneliness.

Mops leaned against his leg, and he reached down to stroke the dog's head.

"We're in the same boat, friend," Scott said. "We've got no home."

Mops whined softly, and Scott kept listening for the sound of Wynne's car. At last, he heard it and left the beach to go meet her.

"How did it go?"

Wynne shook her head tiredly. "I'm worried about her. It seemed like the fight went out of her. I hadn't expected that."

"She's done her share of fighting in her day," Scott pointed out. "There comes a time when it's just too much effort—my grandfather was like that. He fought all kinds of problems on his Wyoming ranch. Drought. Blizzards. Starving cattle. Poor markets. Real hardship. But he stood up for a long, long time. Then, something happened, and the fight was gone."

Wynne put a hand on his arm. "Thanks for waiting up for me, Scott. I dreaded coming back here. Oh, Scott—"

144

He gathered her swiftly into his arms. He held her close, and for a moment, she clung to him. He wanted to protect her. He wanted to do something about the bridge that was making her so unhappy. Oh, if only he could. If there was some way he could show her how much he loved her! But he couldn't bring himself to offer her any kind of false hope. The bridge was going to be a fact. There was no stopping it now.

"Would you like to go for a ride? Have something at the Hurricane? Take a walk?"

"A walk," she said. "I need the fresh air. I need time to get used to the whole idea."

Mops was told to stay, but when he tried to hobble along with them, Scott went back and picked the dog up in his arms.

"He's getting to be a nuisance," Scott laughed.

"And you love every minute of it."

Scott nodded. "Yes. I suppose it's foolish to be so crazy about a pet. I love this old dog. I hope no one ever claims him."

With Mops under his arm, Scott walked beside Wynne, slowly, watching the surf at their feet. Wynne spoke very little. He didn't press her. It was enough that he was here with her now, that she seemed to need him beside her.

"What will I do, Scott? Shall I try to hang on to the South Wind, even when my good sense tells me that I'll never be able to compete? Updating the hotel would cost a fortune, and would it be worth it?"

Scott paused and put the dog down. He turned Wynne to face him. "You haven't forgotten what I told you the other night, have you? I love you, Wynne. I want to marry you. If you want to leave the South Wind and come with me, I know I'd make you happy."

She touched his face for a moment with cool fingers. "You're sweet, Scott. But I'm not even sure I can leave the South Wind. I've got my hang-up too."

"If you'd ask me, I'd stay. I'd help you. I'd do everything in my power—"

She leaned toward him and kissed his lips gently. "Thank you. But it wouldn't be fair. I couldn't do that to you, Scott, or anyone."

145

He felt his throat go dry, and a kind of thudding started up inside his chest. It was still Eric Channon. Perhaps it always would be.

"Wynne, I just want you to be happy. I want that more than anything."

"Only a few weeks ago, I didn't know you, Scott. Now here you are sharing some of the most important moments of my life."

"I'd like to share them all," he said gently. "Darling, whatever you decide, I'm sure it's going to be the right thing."

She took his arm, and they walked on. Mops grew drowsy under Scott's arm. They returned to the hotel at last, and Wynne told him good-night.

He left Mops in the car and went up to his room. But he could not sleep. Finally, he got up and sat by the window and looked out to the sea. When the phone rang, it startled him. He leaped up to answer it.

"Scott, it's Grandmother! I've just had a call from Wilma. She's very ill. I must take her to the doctor at Charlton. Will you come with me?"

"I'll be right down."

He flew into his clothes and rushed down the steps. Wynne was waiting for him in the lobby, her smoky gray eyes wide with fear, her slender hands wrung together.

They rushed out into the night, and Scott took the wheel. He drove very fast, as fast as he dared up the twisting narrow road.

The Russell house was ablaze with lights. Wynne rushed ahead of him, and Wilma came to open the door.

Scott had never been inside the house before. Impressions rushed out at him. The smell of cleaning wax, the salt air, a mixture of formal and informal, all very well kept, all comfortable and pleasing to the eye. Wynne had disappeared, but was back in a moment.

"I've phoned Sam, he'll be waiting to take us across," Wynne said. "Grandmother's ready to travel, but I don't want her to walk, to exert herself—"

"I'll carry her," Scott said.

Wynne led him into the bedroom. Priscilla Russell's eyes were glazed, and she was having trouble breathing. The shock of the bridge? Scott bent over her.

"Hello, Mrs. Russell," he said gently. "I'm Scott Stoner. A friend of your granddaughter's. Could you put your arms around my neck? I'm going to give you a free ride to the car."

The old lady's eyes registered gratitude. A faint smile touched her lips.

"You remind me of my husband, years ago," she said. "He was big and tall like you."

"Grandmother, don't talk," Wynne said. "Save your strength."

Scott picked up Priscilla Russell in his arms, surprised to find that she weighed so little, that she was so tiny.

Gently, carefully, Scott carried her out to the car. Wynne made her comfortable there, and then, he got behind the wheel again. He wasted no time in driving to the dock. Sam was waiting, the chain down, the ferry ready to move into action.

They bounced on board, and in a matter of seconds, Sam had them under way. Scott left the car for a moment to speak with him.

"Give it all you've got, Sam. Mrs. Russell is a pretty sick lady."

"Full steam," Sam nodded. "Too bad. She's a grand old lady, Scott. One of the best. They don't make them like that anymore. I phoned ahead. An ambulance will be waiting."

"Bless you, Sam."

Scott had never known Sam to make the crossing in such short time. With a sense of relief, Scott saw the lights of Charlton drawing near. A few minutes later, they were tied up at the dock, and Mrs. Russell was being put aboard the ambulance. Scott and Wynne followed in the car.

Wynne's cheeks were streaked with tears. But she had not shed any in front of her grandmother. It must have taken a bit of doing.

"She'll be all right," Scott said. "I'm sure she will."

"But everything's against her. Everything!"

Scott squeezed her hand and could find nothing comforting to say. It seemed to take a long while to reach the hospital. Then at last, he saw the large building and parked the car. Wynne rushed inside, and Scott followed.

There was nothing they could do but wait. Then at last, the doctor came to see them. He looked grave.

"It's a heart condition. Has she had some kind of shock?"

"Yes. A very personal matter, something about which she felt deeply," Wynne said.

"We'll keep her hospitalized and run a few tests. We'll give her the necessary medication and see that she rests comfortably."

"Will she be all right?"

The doctor hesitated. "Frankly, Miss Russell, it's too soon to tell."

Wynne seemed to sag, and Scott put his arm around her.

"May I see her?" Wynne asked.

"Just for a few minutes."

"I'd like to stay the night with her."

"It's not necessary, Miss Russell. Or advisable. We don't want to worry her, and if she thought she was so seriously ill that you felt you must stay—well, you understand."

Scott went with Wynne up to the third floor and paused at the door as Wynne stepped in.

"Grandmother," he heard Wynne say.

"Where's that nice young man?" she asked.

Scott smiled and stepped into view. "I'm right here, Mrs. Russell. Is there something I can do for you?"

"Yes," she nodded. "Take this girl back to the island. I'm all right."

Scott exchanged a glance with Wynne and nodded. "If you say so. In a few minutes. Now be a good patient and do as the doctors say, promise?"

She tried to smile again. "I promise. Will you come back to see me?"

"You can be sure of that," Scott said.

He stepped out to let Wynne say good-bye in private. In a few moments, Wynne joined him, and they silently took the elevator down to the hospital lobby. Just as wordlessly, they drove to the dock where Sam was waiting.

"She looks so frail. So small. So—worn—" Wynne burst out.

Scott held Wynne's hand for a moment tightly in his own. But he couldn't find anything to say.

Sam got the ferry under way, and they joined him at the wheel. He asked several questions about Priscilla Russell and seemed truly concerned.

"Wynne, you ought to tell your father about this, Sam said.

"I'm not sure where he is, Sam. By now, he's probably left Miami."

"He's still there. I heard from him the other day. I've got his address and a phone number at home. I'll give it to you."

When they reached Feather Island, Sam went inside his office to get the information for Wynne and wrote it on a slip of paper.

They drove down the narrow road to the Gulf side of the island, and Wynne got quickly out of the car.

"It's very late, but I'm going to try and reach Dad tonight," she said.

"Good idea," Scott said.

"Perhaps. I don't know. Dad was so bitter when he left. Grandmother too. I'm not sure he should come to see her. But I'll tell him. I must do that."

Scott saw her into her apartment. "If there's anything else, Wynne, anything I can do—"

"You've been so kind, so considerate, Scott. And Grandmother likes you! It's not often she takes an instant liking to anyone."

Scott smiled. "Then I feel honored." He kissed her for a brief moment. Then he let her go and closed the door behind him. He walked out to the beach for a moment and looked up at the stars. The skies didn't seem as bright or as clear. The air wasn't as fresh. If he didn't miss his guess, a storm was building up out there in the Gulf.

XXIV

THE FIRST THING the next morning, Wynne made a phone call to the hospital. The nurse in charge refused to let her speak with her grandmother.

"Is she worse?" Wynne asked with alarm.

"She's sleeping. I don't want to disturb her. If there's any change at all, I promise we'll be in touch. We have your number."

"Thank you. Please tell her I phoned."

Wynne hung up with an empty, aching feeling. She tried again to reach her father, but he was out. She left a message.

She tried to concentrate on the work at hand. There was talk of a storm building up out in the Gulf, but she couldn't think about it just now.

During the afternoon, she made a quick visit to Charlton. Grandmother seemed weaker. Tired. She talked very little and worried about who was minding the desk at the hotel.

It was with reluctance that Wynne went home. Still, there was no word from her father.

She stayed in the office, trying to concentrate on paper work. At ten, Edward closed the desk and disappeared. In one of the desk drawers, Wynne found the note that Lorrie was supposed to have left her. Why would someone do such a thing? Perhaps Brad was right. Someone had wanted her to find the scarf.

Scott appeared in the doorway.

"You're working very late."

"Where have you been all day?"

"Business in Charlton. I dropped by the hospital before I came back. Your grandmother was glad to see me. You know, she's a great gal. I took her some flowers."

"Scott, you were such a help to me last night. Perhaps you can help me with something else."

"Just name it."

She studied the note for a few moments. It was the typescript that seemed so strange. Not like any typewriter she had ever used, or for that matter, like any typewriter she'd ever seen.

Then with a quick frown, she was remembering Edward's typewriter. The one she'd seen in his room. A foreign model. Could it be—

"Darling, what is it? You look so frightened!" Scott said.

She told him the entire story. Scott stared at her with a stunned expression.

"It's only a theory. One that Brad and I have pieced together. We could be dead wrong. Perhaps we weren't meant to find the purse or the scarf or even the car."

"And this note was all part of the plot?" Scott asked.

"Scott, I want you to come with me. To Edward Allen's room. He's gone out. I saw him drive away in his car a few minutes ago."

She went to get the master key to the hotel rooms, and with Scott beside her, they walked quietly up the stairs and down the hall. It was not late, but George Laughlin and the Wilkin twins always retired early. The Grants had gone out and not yet returned. Diane Carlson's typewriter was going noisily.

At Edward's door, Wynne knocked lightly and called his name. There was no answer. She knocked again.

"No one there," Scott said.

With trembling fingers, she used her master key and unlocked the door. She flipped on a light. The bed had not been turned down. Wynne wasted no time. She went straight to the typewriter, put in a fresh sheet of paper and typed a few words. It took only a moment to know that the typing was the same as that on the note.

"But why?" she asked with a puzzled frown. "Why would Edward lure me to Twin Palms—"

Scott had found the locked closet. "I have a feeling we should see what's inside."

"I have no key," Wynne said. "And I have no right—"

Scott gave her a quick grin. "As proprietor of this

151

hotel, you have every right to make a safety inspection. What if the wiring inside is bad? It could cause a fire."

Wynne gave him a nervous smile. "But how do we open it?"

Scott reached up into Wynne's hair and took out a bobby pin. Bending it into a straight wire, he bent to the task.

"I learned this from an old locksmith I knew. It looks like a simple lock."

In a few minutes, she was startled to see the door come open. Scott flipped on the closet light.

"Well, well!" he murmured. "Interesting."

In the corner stood a rifle outfitted with a telescopic lens.

"I can't believe it," Wynne said. "Why? Why would he shoot at Brad and Johnny—"

Carefully, Scott returned the rifle to its hiding place in the corner of the closet. Taking her arm, Scott hurried her out of the room and down the hall.

"I must tell Max about this," Wynne said. "We shouldn't wait any longer."

Two days before, Max had received a third note. It was explicit. Terrifying. The money was to be left at Twin Palms in a briefcase. He had already decided it was foolish to do anything but deliver the cash. There was too much at stake.

Even owning the bank in Charlton made it difficult to get the money together on such short notice. He did it all as quietly as possible. In the same manner, he purchased a pistol.

He ate no dinner that evening, despite Mattie's scolding. For a while, he stepped out to the balcony. The night air seemed oppressive.

The hands on his watch crawled along. Then at twenty minutes of eleven, Max left the house. He got into his car and drove slowly down the road. Twin Palms was not far. Before he reached it, he pulled his car under the trees where it was not visible from the road. Then carefully, quietly, he made his way into the palm trees and looked about. No one was there. The picnic grounds looked very empty and lonely. Once he whirled about, certain he'd heard someone behind him. But there was nothing. He was cold one moment, hot the next. His hands were shaking. Then, as he was directed, he hid the briefcase in the spot specified, covered it with sand and left quickly, not looking back.

He was certain he was being watched. It was only common sense that told him so. With this in mind, he got into his car, turned it around, and sped away swiftly. He wouldn't have much time. Once he was around a bend in the road, he again pulled off and hid the car the best he could. Touching the pistol in his pocket, he began running back through the brush and the trees in the direction of Twin Palms.

When he drew near, he slowed down, mindful of any sound he might make. His breath was raspy and thundering in his ears. He was drenched with sweat. He took up a hiding place and waited. From there, he could see the exact spot where the money was, and he could tell that it had not yet been disturbed.

He hunched his knees under his chin and wrapped his arms around his legs. The pistol in his hand, a powerful flashlight in his pocket. With his back against a tree, he waited.

Scott and Wynne left the hotel with Scott at the wheel of Wynne's car. The road to the Hethershaw house was a winding one. But somehow, Scott swung the car around the twisting curves with ease and speed.

As they passed Twin Palms, Scott suddenly swerved over to the side of the road and stopped.

"I saw Edward's car back there. Under the trees. Let's have a look."

Scott took Wynne's hand, and they hurried along the dark road, moving quietly. Wynne thought surely this was all happening in a nightmare. But Scott's hand was warm and firm around hers. Her hair stuck damply to her neck, and her face felt warm and flushed.

"Easy now," Scott said.

They had reached Twin Palms, and Scott pulled her under a tree and pressed her close to the curved trunk.

"Edward's up there," Scott whispered hoarsely. "He's digging in the sand."

153

"Planting more of Ilsa's belongings?"

"Sh!" Scott cautioned. "He's coming this way."

Then suddenly, the night was brilliant with the strong beam of a flashlight. Edward was pinned in the glare, startled, a briefcase in his hand. He burst into a run. Pistol shots rang out, kicking up the sand just in front of him.

"Stop right there!" a voice shouted. "The next one will catch you in the chest!"

Edward came to a halt, looking from side to side, trying to escape the blinding light.

"Drop the briefcase, Edward."

Wynne knew the voice. She gripped Scott's arm. "It's Max!"

They watched as the light bobbed up and down as Max moved toward Edward. The briefcase lay in the sand at Edward's feet.

"All right, where is she?" Max demanded with a voice made of iron.

Edward laughed in an insulting way. "We both know where she is, don't we? I know what you've done with her."

"You know nothing of the kind," Max said in an even voice. "Because I've done nothing to Ilsa. You are the man she was meeting, aren't you? I knew there was someone!"

"It won't track, Max," Edward said in an ugly voice. "When I tell them what I know, no one will believe you. You couldn't handle Ilsa. She was too much for you. So in a fit of temper, you killed her, put her in the little red car, and sent her over the edge at Sunset Point."

"I've never harmed a hair on Ilsa's head," Max said. "And if you have, I'll make you pay, here and now!"

Edward laughed again. Wynne couldn't believe what she was seeing and hearing.

"You don't dare pull the trigger, Max," Edward said. "If you do, how will you ever know if Ilsa is alive or not? Or where she is? Is she at the bottom of the ocean or in London or Italy or just Miami? You don't dare pull the trigger."

"Then, I'll take you in, and you can tell the police," Max said.

"OK, let's go," Edward said. "Going to leave all that money laying there in the sand?"

Max bent to pick it up, trying to juggle the pistol, flashlight, and briefcase all at the same time. It was the exact moment Edward was waiting for. He leaped on Max, and they began to struggle.

Wynne screamed as a pistol shot blasted the night. Scott ran. The flashlight was knocked aside, and Wynne went to retrieve it. In a moment, Edward was down in the sand, breathing hard. Max and Scott stood over him.

Edward sat up dazed.

"Who are you?" Max demanded. "Where is Ilsa?"

Edward laughed bitterly. "You never bothered to meet Ilsa's family, what little she had," he said. "Otherwise you'd know who I am. I'm Ilsa's stepbrother. I wanted money to start up a new hotel on the island. Feather Island's going to boom when the bridge comes, and I want a piece of the action."

"Ilsa's stepbrother!" Max exclaimed.

"It was you that concocted the idea of putting Ilsa's car over at Sunset Point. It was you that hid the scarf and the purse," Wynne said.

"We found your rifle," Scott said evenly. "You fired on Brad's boat."

"Sure, sure!" Edward said angrily. "I knew that would get Brad real curious, and he'd go back for a look. That's what I wanted. I wanted people to suspect. The more pressure I could put on Hethershaw, the better I'd like it. So high and mighty—got pockets lined with money!"

Max reached out to grab Edward by the shirt. "Where's Ilsa?" he shouted angrily.

"What do you care?" Edward snarled. "She helped me set this up. She thought it was a big joke on you. That's how much she thinks of you, Max Hethershaw!"

"I want to know where she is!"

"Having a ball in Miami," Edward grinned. "I've been keeping her up to date on the action. We've had lots of laughs over it. She won't be coming back here again."

Max backed away, shoulders sagging. His face was a picture of agony as he contemplated the truth. He was a man who had just taken the ultimate beating. Edward's rough laughter only made it worse.

155

Scott had retrieved the pistol. He motioned to Edward with it. "My car's just up the road. Max, will you phone the police or shall we?"

Max stood very quietly for a moment. He stared at Edward, clutching the briefcase tightly in his hand.

"No police," Max said quietly. "Let him go."

"But, Max—" Wynne said.

"Just get off the island before morning, Edward," Max said with steel in his voice. "I don't want to see you again."

XXV

BY THE TIME Wynne and Scott returned to the hotel, Edward Allen was gone. Wynne didn't know when or where. She only knew his room was cleared and the door left standing open.

Next morning, over breakfast at Ruby's place, Wynne told Brad and Lorrie what had happened.

"What an incredible story!" Brad said.

"Not really so incredible," Lorrie shook her head. "You didn't know Ilsa. She was a will-o'-the-wisp. Yet, there was a hard core inside her too. I'm sure she thought the whole thing was just a lark. She liked to torment Max. Only this time, she went too far."

Ruby appeared with the coffeepot to refill their cups.

"Have you heard the warnings? A hurricane is definitely heading our way. I just heard it on the radio."

Wynne's heart began to knock. "How soon?"

"We've got about eight hours to get ready."

"A bad one?" Brad asked anxiously.

"Listen, honey," Ruby said. "Anytime that wind begins to howl on Feather Island, it's bad!"

Wynne quickly finished her coffee. "I've got to get back. We have a great deal to do."

Returning to the South Wind, she found Marge and Pete waiting for her. They too had heard the warnings.

"We're in for a big blow," Pete said.

"Marge, set up some emergency cots in the basement for the guests, with first aid supplies, jugs of water, and some food. Just in case. If I can, I'll try to get everyone to evacuate," Wynne said. "Pete, handle things outside."

There was always so much to be done. Wynne had seen her father prepare for such storms. Sometimes, the preparations had been in vain. Storms changed courses

157

or blew out before they reached the island. But Wynne knew she couldn't take any chance. They would have to prepare the best they could.

She took time to make two phone calls. One to her father, who still could not be reached, and another to the hospital.

Grandmother's condition was unchanged.

The radio spat out new warnings every few minutes. The path of the storm was being closely watched. As the day shortened, it was apparent that they were going to catch the brunt of the storm.

Scott had been helping Pete all day. They had carried in all the beach chairs and tables and umbrellas. They had boarded the windows and fastened the awnings down tight. Every conceivable preparation had been made to protect the hotel. But would it be enough?

The broken window had never been repaired. Perhaps it was just as well the carpenter had been delayed in coming to fix it.

All day, the entire island had been in a state of alarm. A few boarded up their houses and simply left the island, preferring to ride out the storm in Charlton. Scott and Pete had gone up in the middle of the morning and made Grandmother's house as secure as possible.

Most of the hotel guests left. Wynne saw them safely to the ferry to Charlton. But since George Laughlin had decided to stay, the Wilkin twins wouldn't leave either. It was still one more of their childish games, but Wynne had neither the will nor the time to put an end to it.

It was evening when Wynne heard people coming into the hotel lobby. Always before, her father had offered a haven to anyone who cared to come. She went to find Johnny and Lorrie with Brad close behind them.

"Brad helped us button up the house," Johnny said.

"Where's your father?" Wynne asked.

"Dad's gone," Lorrie said.

"What do you mean, gone?"

"He left the island. For good. Can you imagine that? I'm not sure what happened. I think there was trouble with Max Hethershaw. I don't know what. He wouldn't tell me. Every time I asked, he just got angry."

"What about you and Johnny?"

"As soon as I can, I'll find us a place on the mainland. We'll be leaving the island too."

Ruby Hammer arrived next and then Benson. Benson stood in the doorway for a moment, as if uncertain.

"Come in," Wynne said. "There's always room for one more."

Benson seemed reluctant to come inside. He kept eyeing the broken front window.

"Miss Russell, I've got to apologize," he said. "I don't know what got into me. I swear, I don't. I'll pay for a new one. You get it fixed and send me the bill."

"You mean you—"

"Yes. I'm the one who broke the window. Every time I thought about the survey crew up here, I wanted to do something. Might as well have just accepted it. I heard the bridge is a sure thing now."

"It's starting!" someone shouted. "The wind's starting."

The Wilkin twins were nervously talking with each other. George strutted around as if he were defying the storm to hit. All the others were trying to sit quietly, trying not to listen to the roar of the wind.

The door came open again, and Wynne saw Eric. Her heart skipped a beat. She had not expected him to come.

"Do you mind?" he asked.

"Of course not. Is there anything new about the storm?"

"Only that it's picked up in speed. It's coming faster than they expected."

Eric was watching her closely. The air was growing heavier by the minute in the stuffy lobby. All windows had been sealed and shuttered. But Wynne didn't think this was why she found it hard to breathe. It was the danger and excitement of the storm, coupled with the presence of Eric.

The phone was ringing. Lorrie hurried to answer it.

"Miss Russell, this is the hospital."

The heart went right out of her. "What's happened? How is my grandmother?"

"She's taken a turn for the worse. We realize the weather is bad, but if you could come—"

Wynne hung up. For a paralyzed moment or two, she couldn't move. Then with a sob, she ran out to the lobby and toward the door.

"Wynne, what is it?" Scott said. He came running after her. "You can't go out. The wind's starting!"

"It's Grandmother. I must go to her."

Scott shook his head. "Darling, it's too dangerous."

The tears were burning her eyes and streaking her cheeks. Scott shook her, trying to make her see reason. But all she could think of was Grandmother.

The door flung open, and Captain Sam came in, his yellow slicker wet with rain. Then Wynne saw the tall man with him.

"Dad!"

"I finally got your message. I came right away. I heard about the hurricane. Are you ready? Is there anything I can do?"

Wynne gripped her father's arm. "Dad, I just had a call from the hospital. It's Grandmother. She's worse. They want me to come."

"Out of the question, girl!" Sam said. "You can't take a boat out on the water. I couldn't risk the ferry."

"But I *must* go!"

Dad looked at her for a moment. He shook his head. "No. You stay here. Where you belong. I'll go. I—I don't know if she'll let me in the room, but I'll go—"

"Dad—" Wynne went to him and gave him a quick kiss. "Be careful. Please, be careful."

"I've got the small boat with the fifty horse," Sam was saying. "We'll take that. Don't fret, Wynne, I'll get him there."

"Oh, be careful. Please—"

She watched them go out into the driving wind and rain. Could they possibly make it across the sound before the main force of the storm hit the island?

Eric appeared beside her. His eyes were compassionate. He touched her hand. "Don't you think you should get everyone below?"

She forced herself to think about the hotel and her guests and all the people who had come here for shelter.

"Yes. You're right. Take them down, will you, Eric? I'll be there in a moment or two."

When they had all gone down to the basement, Wynne walked around the lobby one last time. The wind was tearing at the hotel now. Through a crack in the shutters

160

she saw the angry sea churning, billowing green and white, the waves growing higher and higher as they crashed against the shore.

Downstairs, Scott was busy helping make everyone comfortable. He carefully avoided her eyes. Mops was hobbling about, whining. Lorrie and Brad were huddled together, talking. And the wind blew.

There was the sound of shattering wood above, and all of them leaped to their feet in alarm. Wynne felt the blood drain out of her face. Had part of the building been ripped away? Then there was a loud crash that seemed to jar them all.

"A tree came down," Eric guessed. "One of the palms out in front."

Wynne took a flashlight and checked around the basement floor, checking for leaks. Her nerves were stretched tight. Her mind was torn in two ways, one part following her father and Sam to the hospital across the dangerous sound, the other right here, listening to the old hotel creak and groan in the wind, struggling to stay alive.

The lights went out. Wynne had seen to it that there was an ample supply of candles. They lighted a few of them, and it gave the place an eeriness.

Nettie Wilkin fainted. Poor Lettie was beside herself. But surprisingly, it was George Laughlin who took command of the situation.

"She's just scared, poor thing," George said. "Wynne, bring me a cold cloth. Or some smelling salts, if you've got them."

In a few minutes, Nettie opened her eyes and found herself practically in George's arms. She stared at him with wonder.

"You fainted," George said gruffly. "Now, just lie still. You're going to be all right. Don't let the storm worry you. We're safe here."

"Why, George!" Nettie said with wonder. "How nice you are!"

George coughed, embarrassed. Lettie hid a giggle behind her hand.

And still the storm raged. Everyone had grown quiet, listening, fearing what they would hear next.

Eric came to sit down beside Wynne. He took her hand in his. "Are you all right?"

"Yes."

"It's a hell of a break," he said. "First the bridge, now this. And your grandmother . . ."

The sympathy in his voice touched her heart. She felt warmed by it. He gave her a smile, and her spirits lifted. It was the first time since she had returned that they had not quarreled when they met.

"I do care, you know," Eric said. "I'm not as cold and insensitive as you think."

"No. You're not."

Eric leaned toward her, his sea green eyes studying her.

"Look, can we be friends again?"

She nodded. "Yes. We can be friends, Eric. At least we can be friends."

"It's letting up!" someone said. "I think the wind's passed over!"

They listened closely, anxiously. The hotel had grown almost quiet. With a rush, Wynne hurried up the steps and into the lobby. Scott and Eric were right behind her.

A corner of the hotel was gone. Rain was pouring in, drenching the Persian carpeting. The front of the hotel looked as if it had been twisted on its foundation.

With a cry, Wynne went outside. The sand stung her face, and the rain soaked her to the skin, but she had to see. Palm trees were down or the tops broken off of them. The hotel looked as if it had been grasped by a huge hand. Siding had buckled. Window frames were squeezed out. The roof sagged precariously.

Eric shook his head. "It will never stand a safety inspection. You'll have to get everyone out. They can't stay here any longer."

Wynne covered her face with her hands for a moment. The sea was quieting. The waves were growing smaller, receding. Litter was everywhere on the beach. The breakers had reached as far as the veranda, and some of it had been torn away too.

"It's all over," Wynne said. "All over."

Scott came to stand before her. "Why don't you come in now?"

She clutched his arms with cold fingers. "Find a fast boat. Take me to the mainland. I have to see Grandmother now. Please!"

Inside the hotel, George had taken command. Wynne explained that they would all have to leave, that none of them would be allowed into their rooms until they had been inspected for safety.

"You can come to my place," Ruby Hammer said. "I was lucky. Just a few broken windows. Come along, folks, I'll fix you something to eat. I think we could all use a strong cup of coffee."

When the hotel guests had gone next door and the others had hurried away to check their own properties, Scott helped Wynne into his car, and they drove down to the dock. Some of it had been broken up, but on the bay side the damage was never as bad as on the Gulf side. Scott found a boat that seemed seaworthy, and with a pull of a rope, the motor started.

It was a rough, choppy ride across the sound, but Scott handled the boat competently, and when they had reached the other side, he asked the police for an escort to the hospital.

It was a long half hour before Wynne found herself rushing into the hospital and up to the third floor. Grandmother's door was closed. She twisted the knob, her heart thundering, and stepped in.

Dad looked up. He sat beside Grandmother's bed, holding her hand tightly in his.

"Dad!"

Grandmother heard her. She turned her head ever so slightly, trying to see her.

"Wynne—the hotel—the storm—"

She didn't know what to say. She leaned over the old lady, and no words were necessary. Grandmother saw in her face what had happened.

Grandmother nodded. "Yes. Of course. It's all over for the South Wind. And for me."

Wynne looked with alarm to her father, and he shook his head slowly.

A few minutes later, barely an hour since the South Wind had groaned and creaked under the last of the wind, Priscilla Russell died as well.

XXVI

THE NEXT FEW DAYS were chaos for Wynne. They were filled with grief and sorrow for the loss of her grandmother. The house and the hotel had been left to her. But she was not sure she could bear to stay on the island. George Laughlin and the Wilkin twins found accommodations at Charlton and decided to spend the rest of the summer there. George had become the old girls' protector, and he seemed proud of his new role. Diane Carlson closed her typewriter and stole away. The Grants departed on the first plane out of Charlton.

Dad stayed long enough to help her with Grandmother's estate.

"Will you be all right?" he wanted to know the day he left.

"Yes."

"What will you do, Wynne?"

"I don't know. The important thing is that you and Grandmother—"

Dad lowered his head. "Yes. When the chips were down, we stuck. All the old quarrels and misunderstandings, all the bitterness and anger were gone. Why don't you come with me? Travel for a while."

She shook her head. "No. I'll stay. I must decide what to do."

Dad smiled. "And you'll do it. Like your grandmother would have done it. You're a Russell, all right. No doubt about it."

She drove him down to Captain Sam's. The ferry had been damaged, but it was repairable. Sam would take Dad across in a small boat.

"Look after her for me, Sam," Dad said.

"You can bet on that!" Captain Sam grinned. "You just be careful out there in the winds of the West."

Wynne stood on the shore, waving, until they were barely visible.

When she returned to the hotel, Brad was waiting for her. He'd been staying on at the hotel, despite the warnings that the place was no longer considered safe. Scott had gone for a few days on a business matter, but had promised to be back in a week or so.

Over coffee at Ruby's, Brad told her of his plans.

"Under the circumstances, I think I'll cut my vacation short and go back to North Dakota."

"No more diving?"

"I didn't find it anyway."

"What do you mean?"

Brad gave her a wry smile. "I didn't come just to make a few random dives. I was looking for something. I have reason to believe there's an old Spanish galleon lost off the coast of Feather Island. I wanted to find her. Think of the artifacts I could have taken off her!"

"Oh, Brad—what a dreamer you are!"

"I believed it was there. I still do. Who knows, maybe I'll come back next year for another look."

Brad reached out to take her hand in his.

"Wynne, you know I'm very fond of you, don't you? Why not come to North Dakota with me."

"Thank you, Brad. But no. If you really want to invite someone, why don't you ask Lorrie?"

"Lorrie!"

"Oh, Brad, you can spend hours looking for a sunken old ship, but can't take five minutes to look at a girl and see the love in her eyes."

Brad stared at her. "Lorrie? You mean Lorrie—"

Wynne nodded. "I know Lorrie as well as anyone, and I think she's in love with you."

"I'll be damned! I can't believe it. I mean—"

He got quickly to his feet. "Wynne, would you excuse me? I think I see Lorrie on the beach—"

He was gone. From the window of the Hurricane, Wynne watched Brad running across the sand, waving and shouting. Lorrie stopped and turned about. Then

Brad reached her. They talked for a few minutes. As Wynne watched, Brad caught Lorrie up into his big arms and kissed her. They walked away together, arms around each other. Wynne turned away feeling happy and sad. Happy for Lorrie, sad for herself.

What would she do now? Which way did she turn? She had Grandmother's house. It was of real value and had escaped any major damage. But the hotel—the poor gallant old South Wind Hotel—what could she do about it? It would cost a fortune to repair, and when she had finished, it would still be just an old hotel fixed over. And the bridge was coming. With it would come all the changes.

Perhaps she should just pack up and go. Like Will Dykes, she would desert the island. She could go back to Tallahassee. Look up Jack Brown. Get her old job back. What waited for her here but heartache and trouble?

Max Hethershaw had survived the hurricane, and his house had proved strong in the wind. The next few days he stayed in his den. He opened the briefcase and looked at the money inside. How much of it had been Ilsa's share? Didn't she know that all she had to do was ask and he would have given her anything she wanted?

The next few days, the island began putting itself back together. He heard about Priscilla Russell and went down to pay his personal respects to Wynne and her father. He offered his assistance in any way it was needed. If it shocked Harvey Russell, Max wasn't surprised. They had always been on the other side of the fence. Enemies in a way. Yet, Wynne had come to warn him about Edward. For that, he would be eternally grateful to the girl. When it came time to rebuild the South Wind, if she did, he would see that she got all the loan she needed at his bank.

He'd also heard that Will Dykes had gone, even before the hurricane, like a rat scurrying from a sinking ship.

It was the only thought that could bring a smile to Max's lips these days. Will had been blackmailing him in one small way or another about Ilsa. But there was nothing now that Will knew about Ilsa that he didn't. He'd sent the man packing. With a few strong threats thrown in for good measure, and typically, Will Dykes had gone running. The worm had turned.

With the hurricane gone, the weather turned particularly fine. The sun flooded the balcony. The sea was very calm. He didn't go to Charlton, even though he knew there were pressing matters waiting for him at the bank. He stayed at home, on the balcony, watching the ships on the horizon.

It was late one afternoon when he heard her steps. He didn't move or turn around. She came to lean on the railing of the balcony and at last turned to face him.

"Hello, Max."

"What is it you want now?" he asked.

"You're angry."

He laughed bitterly. "You must think I'm a terrible fool, Ilsa. Did you expect me to fall on my knees at the mere sight of you?"

Ilsa was lovely. Always so lovely. He tried not to think about that. He looked down at his hands.

"It was nice to meet your stepbrother, at last," he said.

"Max, about the—"

He lifted his head. She stopped talking and went pale.

"He was your brother. Your only family. Did it ever occur to you just to ask me for the money to loan him?"

Ilsa stared at him.

"Was it so much fun to trick and threaten me?" Max asked. "How much of the hundred thousand was to be yours?"

"None of it!" Ilsa replied quickly. "None of it. It was all Edward's idea."

"But you went along with it. You encouraged it."

Ilsa gripped the railing tightly. "Would you believe I did it for kicks? For fun? It gave me something to think about. A little excitement."

Max said nothing.

"Will you forgive me?"

Max said nothing. He stared out to the sea. In a moment, Ilsa straightened. He could smell her perfume. A silky scarf fluttered in the breeze. He closed his eyes for a moment.

"Do you want me to go?" Ilsa asked.

He couldn't reply. She came to him and touched his arm for a moment.

"I'm sorry. I've been stupid and childish. Maybe worse. Edward always had this crazy power over me. I always did what he wanted. I don't know why."

He still did not answer. She took her hand away.

"Would you believe I want to stay, Max? It's funny, when something's gone, you know how much it meant. I do love you, Max, despite everything."

Then with a sob, she walked away, her steps echoing back to him. He got slowly to his feet.

"Ilsa—"

She paused to look back at him. His lovely Ilsa. His blood was singing through his veins for the first time in days. He reached out his hand.

"Ilsa—"

She came running back to him, dark hair flying. Then she was in his arms, all the lovely soft scent of her, and he was whole again. He was alive. Nothing else mattered.

XXVII

THE HOTEL was boarded up. What could be saved was salvaged and stored. Wynne moved into her grandmother's house and like Grandmother, spent long hours on the veranda, staring at the sea, trying to decide what to do.

Scott spent many evenings there with her. They talked quietly and grew to know each other. The splint came off Mops's leg, and he was as good as new.

Then one afternoon, there was a knock at the door, and Wynne went to answer it. Jack Brown stood there, smiling at her.

"Jack! What on earth are you doing here?"

"I came to hire you," Jack said.

"My old job?" she asked.

"Not exactly. You'd be working here on Feather Island."

"I don't understand."

"The hotel that Scott staked out will be built and operated by us. I'd like you to help manage it."

She stared at him with surprise. "You mean Scott works for you?"

"No. Not really. He was hired only for this one job. I'm surprised you didn't know who he was. You must have seen each other in Tallahassee at the office."

She nodded. "So, that's why he seemed familiar! I suppose I did, but I didn't know who he was."

"How about it, Wynne? It would be good to work together again."

"You've heard about the South Wind, I suppose."

"Yes. And I'm sorry. I know you had deep ties to the old hotel. But this is a new era, Wynne. A new age. A new look is coming to the island. Think about it. I'll be in touch again."

On that note he left her. She was all the more be-
wildered now. But Jack had opened a door for her. It
would be an easy step through. But could she turn her
back on the old South Wind? Could she become a part
of someone else's hotel?

When Scott came that evening for dinner, they ate on
the veranda and watched the sun go down.

"Wynne, I haven't wanted to press. But I do need to
talk to you, seriously."

He turned his hazel eyes on her, and she saw the gold
specks giving off their tiny lights.

"I have to know something," Scott said. "I couldn't
help but notice during the hurricane that you and Eric—"

She smiled. Eric had been kind. Good. Like the Eric
she had once known. It was good to find an old friend
again.

"Eric's a friend, Scott. Nothing more. Somehow, the
hurricane cleared away a lot of debris in my mind too.
I'm thinking straight for a change."

Scott's face broke into a broad smile. She had never
seen him look so happy.

"I've wanted to hear you say that! You've no idea how
much I wanted that!"

Scott reached out to take her hands in his. "I have news.
I've got a job at Charlton. As an industrial engineer. It
means no traveling around. No more hotel rooms. I can
have a home. A real home!"

"You want that very much, don't you?"

"Only if you share it with me, Wynne."

She looked into his face and saw his heart in his eyes.
She felt warm inside. A little tingly.

"I'm at loose ends, Scott. I don't know where I'm
going or why. I need time. Will you be patient?"

"You know I will."

She thought about her future for the next few days,
hour on end. Finally, she got in her car and drove down
to the site of the new hotel. She walked around, imagin-
ing how it would look. Jack had left her some plans and
architect's drawings. A beauty. Expensive. Fashionable.
Up to date.

Her heart ached when she thought about it. In her
mind, she compared it to the South Wind. That grand

170

old hotel with its shabby charm and its quaint look. Her eyes stung with tears. Oh, it wasn't fair! It wasn't! Why did it have to come to this?

Something had to be done with the hotel. She had to either rebuild it or tear it down. Driving back, she stopped her car and looked at the South Wind. How noble it had been in its day, a grand old lady, just as Grandmother had been a grand old girl. Now, both were gone.

She knew what must be done. There was no reason to delay. She went home and began making phone calls.

Three weeks later, early in the morning, when the sun was kissing the water and the gulls were soaring over the beach and the sandpipers were running at the water's edge, she watched the heavy equipment move in.

The bulldozers roared and grumbled, crunching across the sand. The wrecking ball swung once and walls shattered and plaster crumbled. With every swing of the ball, Wynne's heart seemed to absorb the blow. She watched the Wilkins' suite with the odd-shaped closet come crashing down. The rose wallpaper was a splotch of color through the dust before it too became rubble. The upstairs hall disappeared. Then the bathroom with the porcelain faucets and the faded red carpeting. The old floors burst open and spilled out everything to the ground below.

She saw her cozy little corner disappear in a cloud of dust. Her heart was wrenched. She ached with a loss that was almost unbearable. One memory after another was buried, torn apart, shredded, splintered, broken.

She felt cold even though the sun was hot and bright. Sometime, she didn't really know when, Scott came to stand beside her, saying nothing. Mops sat at their feet, ears twitching with the din.

"They'll never come back."

"Who, darling?" Scott asked gently.

"All the old friends. The twins, George, Dad, dozens and dozens of people who once lived here and loved it and called it home."

"But there will be other people, new people, and in time, they'll love the new hotel as much as the old friends loved the old one. Only this time, *you'll* be a part of their memories. *You'll* really be the hotel."

"I didn't want to tear it down. I don't really want to

build a new hotel. But I can't do anything else, can I?"

Scott smiled. "Being you, no. You can't."

"I'm not doing it for myself. I'm doing it for Grand-mother. I think she would like me to do that."

"No, darling. Not for your grandmother. For you. You can't hang on to yesterday. Let's not watch any longer. Come away."

The bulldozers droned on. The wrecking ball was destroying the South Wind inch by inch. Soon, there would be nothing at all. For a moment, she was filled so with despair that she felt hopelessly lost.

"Oh, Scott, what can I hold on to? What will last?"

He put his arms around her. "Me, darling. My love will last. For the rest of your lifetime."

He smiled at her, and she saw the truth in his eyes. It seemed the noise of the heavy machines faded away. She was aware only of the white sand of the beach, the morning sun on the water. With a rush, she flung her arms around Scott and clung to him.

"Yes, you'll be here. You'll always be here."

Then she kissed him for a long, eager moment.

"I told you, darling, that someday you'd kiss me the way I wanted you to kiss me!"

He held her so close that she could no longer hear the crashing of the South Wind coming down. Just the solid beating of his heart, the thunder of her own, and the unspoken promise of tomorrow.